Dog Biscuits
Book Six of Underdogs

Geonn Cannon

Supposed Crimes LLC • Matthews, North Carolina

www.supposedcrimes.com

This book is typeset in Goudy Old Style.

DOG BISCUITS

Underdogs Series:

Underdogs: the Novel
Beware of Wolf
Dogs of War
Red in Tooth and Claw
Wilder Animals
Dog Biscuits

Coming in 2018:

Kennel Club

Historical Underdogs Novels:

Wolf at the Door
Stag and Hound

CHAPTER ONE

SUNNY DAYS in Seattle weren't as rare as people liked to claim, but they were still something to be treasured. The light broke through the trees overhead to make a mottled pattern on the sidewalk under her sneakers as Ariadne Willow ran. The streets looked different when she ran on two legs, not to mention in the daytime, with her earbuds blasting the Fratellis on her iPod. Usually she was on all fours, in the dead of night, and her mind was fuzzy with wolf thoughts: smell that, chase that, be aware of everything. Recently Dale had been concerned that the only exercise Ari got was when she was the wolf and, even though she explained that it was all the same musculature being worked, she agreed to start jogging.

She did have one condition, however: she wasn't going to run alone.

She looked back and smiled when she saw Dale keeping up with her. She gave her girlfriend a thumbs-up. Dale gave her a middle finger in return. Ari laughed and faced forward again. Dale had said several times that they looked like total opposites when they ran. Ari was tall and slender in Lycra shorts and a tank top, the straps of her sports bra visible underneath. Dale, meanwhile, claimed she looked like a *Cathy* comic brought to life. Ari loved how she looked in her pale green T-shirt and shorts. She may have been slightly shorter and a bit curvier than Ari, but there was absolutely nothing about her Ari would change.

At the bottom of Cherry Hill, not quite the halfway point of their run, Ari stopped on the corner to give Dale the chance to take a breather. Ari had the speed and stamina of a wolf even when she wasn't in *canidae* form, and it wasn't fair of her to expect Dale to keep up with her the entire route. She smiled and held up her hand to signal a break but Dale didn't even slow down. She blew Ari a kiss as she turned north on Twelfth Street.

"Getting tired, puppy?"

Ari's grin widened and she took off in pursuit. She had spoken loud enough to be heard over Ari's earbuds. Dale preferred to run without music but Ari liked using the songs to time herself. Ari purposefully let Dale keep the lead so she could watch the hypnotic bounce of her pigtails as she turned down Pine. They would take the next right and run next to the park because it was a better view than the apartment buildings they would have otherwise been passing.

Dale looked over her shoulder. "If you're not the lead dog, the view is always the same."

"Yeah, but when it's a view like this..."

Dale's laugh was breathless and a little wheezy. She was still getting used to their daily jogs. The route was just over two-point-three miles, from their apartment to the office. There was another circuitous route they used when they needed to have the car at work. Neither of them wore step trackers or any of those little gadgets that would keep a record of how far they'd gone. They didn't need to compete with themselves or anyone else.

The run took about twenty minutes, depending on if they took any rest breaks, and that day they approached the office just before eight. Ari saw the work trucks parked along the curb but assumed whoever it was had been hired by someone else in the building.

She wiped the sweat from her face and held the door open for Dale. "Before long, you'll even be able to keep up with the wolf."

"I'm not quite that quick yet," Dale said, "but I look forward to a footrace."

Ari reached out and stopped Dale from going further. She smelled them as soon as she entered the building but now she could see silhouettes against the fogged glass of their office door. Dale saw them as well and glanced at Ari to see what she should do. Ari held up two fingers and moved closer to the door. She twisted the knob and shoved it open, stepping over the threshold with the same movement, braced to attack or defend based on what happened next.

"What the hell are you doing in my office?"

All three of the men in the office turned to look at her. They were dressed identically in red polo shirts and khakis. One of the men, a blonde with a thin mustache and leathery skin, stepped forward and extended a bear-paw hand.

"You must be Ariadne Willow. Nate, Nate Fogerson of Fogerson Security. How are you doing this morning?"

"I'm waiting for an answer to my question." Ari tried to forget how she was dressed and crossed her arms over her chest. She tried for imposing but doubted she had pulled it off. She was sweaty, sore, and breathless from her run and knew she must look like a crazy woman. "No one hired you."

Fogerson said, "Actually, ma'am, someone did." He produced a tablet computer and poked the screen. He turned it around so she could see the order. "Cecily Parrish arranged for the entire office to get upgraded with our best security."

Dale peeked over Ari's shoulder. "I didn't know anything about this."

Ari didn't need that confirmed; she knew Dale would have brought it up if she'd been aware. She looked over the work order and then looked past Fogerson at the two workmen.

"How much of the work have you already done?"

"I'd say we're a good two-thirds through. Miss Parrish said she wanted it done ASAP and I... well, I really wanted to make her happy, you know?"

"Yeah, I know the feeling," Ari said. "Okay. Might as well finish. Can you go over everything with Dale?"

Fogerson nodded. "Sure, sure."

Dale said, "I assume you're going to have a word with Miss Parrish about all this."

"Oh, I'm going to have a word. I'm going to have many, many words." She kissed Dale's cheek and left, wishing they had taken the car that morning. "Keep an eye on them for me."

"Like a hawk."

Ari looked at the damage done to her office - her safe space, the two rooms where she and Dale went from strangers to lovers - and forced down her urge to bite Fogerson's head off. The man was just doing his job. It wasn't his fault Cecily had acted without permission. There was a much worthier target for her anger, and Ari kept the fires stoked so she would still be breathing smoke when she got to their offices.

The elevator opened on the hushed waiting room of Gilles Girard and Moreau. Everything looked magazine-perfect, polished to a high sheen. The window beside the elevators reflected sunlight off their neighbors to make it seem as if the offices were glowing. Even though she'd taken an Uber home to change into something a bit more presentable than her workout clothes, she still felt uncomfortable in the offices. She was very aware that even the clients, people who were able to afford Cecily Parrish's services, were a good deal wealthier than she would ever be.

She supposed she had been wealthy, for a time. She'd been born into wealth, inheriting a fortune instead of the ability to transform into a wolf. When she discovered her mother had put her through an experimental and insanely dangerous procedure to make her a *canidae*, a decision that caused Ari intense pain for most of her adult life, she'd run away from home. She found her way in the world, opened her own agency and built a life with Dale, all without her mother's help. She knew the safety net was there but she preferred succeeding on her own. She and Dale were doing just fine.

At least, that's how she felt most days. Days when she wasn't looking at a trio of receptionists who probably made three times her salary just answering phones. Ari could probably afford a part of the outfits they were wearing - a blazer, a blouse, one earring - but only if she got very lucky with sales and skipped eating.

The edge of the elevated front desk came up to the center of Ari's chest, or it would have if she approached it. Instead she moved straight for the floor-to-ceiling glass doors that led into the main offices. The receptionist in the center stood and moved to intercept her.

"Please have a seat, Miss Willow, and I'll tell Miss Parrish you're coming."

"Shannon, right?" The woman glanced at her two associates, neither of whom offered any support. She nodded. Ari started to step around her. "I think I'll just go on back."

"Please..." Shannon held her arms out. "This is childish."

Ari said, "I agree. Let me pass."

"If you would just have a seat and I can call Miss Parrish."

"So she can summon me at her leisure? No, she has enough puppets in this office. Don't you think it would be nice if she was caught off-guard once in a while?"

Shannon pressed her lips together.

"Come on, Shannon." Ari whispered, "It would be nice to know there's one person here who isn't a robot."

"If she asks, I was in the bathroom when you showed up."

Ari winked. "Never saw you."

Shannon moved out of the way and Ari went through the doors. The inner offices were all antiseptic and bland prison cells that looked out over various Seattle scenes. The harbor was visible through the office windows to her right. Directly ahead, she saw the Space Needle. She was well-acquainted with the layout of the offices due to the countless staff meetings she'd attended over the past few months. Cecily wanted to establish Ari as a presence in the company so, while attorneys and paralegals prattled on about their progress in various cases, Ari spent her time looking through the conference room's glass walls at the offices.

The door to Cecily's corner office was open. Ari could see her behind the desk as she approached, but her chair was turned to face the window. Ari entered without knocking and took a seat. She folded her arms and waited silently. The room felt normal to her, not that she was sure what it would feel like if anything was wrong. Ari had revealed her true nature as a *canidae* in exchange for Cecily's secret: she was a succubus. Wolves apparently weren't vulnerable to a succubus' charms, but they did suffer something like a contact high. Ari only had to spend a few minutes in Cecily's presence and women would be throwing themselves at her at an alarming rate.

In the time they'd been working together, Ari hadn't noticed anything peculiar about the other woman since, indicating she had some control over her power. It was either that or Ari had become immune to her pheromones. Whatever the reason, she was glad she didn't have to worry about fending off any amorous Seattle lesbians whenever she left the GG&M offices.

Cecily was speaking to someone. "There's absolutely no reason to worry." Ari glanced at the desk and saw the light indicating an open line on the speakerphone. "I'll keep pestering his attorneys. They don't want to take this to court and the deal I've offered is extremely generous. He's just trying to keep his pride intact by not agreeing immediately."

The man on the phone said, "You do sound confident, Miss Parrish."

"I'm positive." She turned to reach for something on the desk.

The only acknowledgement to Ari's presence was a quick flinch of her fingers and her eyes narrowing. "The worst-case scenario is that we do end up in a courtroom. In that event, I have little doubt we'll emerge victorious. I have nothing to fear from their counsel in that situation. No matter what happens, you are the victor. We're only debating how large your payday will be."

The man sighed. "You're right, Miss Parrish."

She smiled. "Of course I am. If you'll excuse me, Andy, I have another issue which requires my attention. Have a good day." She disconnected the call and tried to subdue her smirk. "I presume this means Mr. Fogerson arrived as scheduled."

"No. You don't get to break into my office and act like it was a prank."

"It was merely a business decision, Ariadne. You have been handling issues pertaining to my clients for the past six months and, so long as you're working for this agency, you will be exposed to privileged information. GG&M clients expect the utmost care to be taken with their privacy. My gesture was simply to ensure that they received that same level of security whether their information was here at our offices or across town at yours."

Ari said, "You still could have brought it up."

Cecily shrugged. "I didn't really see the point. You had no responsibility, no debt. The entire thing is being paid for by GG&M. You get nothing but increased protection for your own clients. I apologize for the minor inconvenience of having the installers at your office unannounced."

"Minor," Ari said.

"In the grand scheme of things, yes."

Ari rolled her eyes and pushed herself up out of the chair. "The agency and everything associated with it is mine. From now on, you want to do anything with, for, or to Bitches Investigations, it gets okayed by me first. Understood?"

Cecily met Ari's gaze for the first time since hanging up the phone. "Understood, Miss Willow."

"Fantastic. I went to this expense because your probationary period is nearly over. The Michael Irwin case proved you were valuable enough to make a few concessions in order to procure your services, but time marches on. The partners are very pleased with your work to date, and they would like to discuss a more permanent arrangement."

Ari stood up. "I'm sticking with my demands. I keep the office,

I keep Dale. Anything else is a non-starter."

"We'll negotiate when the time comes."

"I think you'll be shocked at how stubborn I can be."

Cecily grinned and looked at Ari through her lashes. "I think you'll be surprised at how seductive I can be, wolf."

Ari grimaced and left the office. She suppressed a shudder until she was out of sight, moving toward the back of the building rather than to the exit. She passed the break room where a few assistants and first-year associates were hovering over lukewarm coffee and day-old doughnuts. At the very back corner of the GG&M space, next to the emergency exits, there was a nook set aside for the partners. Ari had smelled it every time she came in, the aroma of fresh baked goods and cappuccino. She took a mug off the shelf and, after figuring out the complicated machinery, poured a cup. She added a dash of milk and just a touch of sugar, then fled before she could get busted.

She was nearly to the elevators when someone called out her name. "Willow! Miss Willow. Uh, Ariadne?" The shout came from a man who looked like a primetime drama version of a lawyer. Catalogue handsome, with a perfect jawline, perfectly coiffed black hair, and large doe eyes that made him seem unthreatening. He was coming out of an office, hurrying around his desk with his arm out like he was hailing a cab. "Sorry. Do you have a minute?"

"Um." She looked down at the coffee.

"I'll be quick. Are you here taking an assignment from Ms. Parrish?"

"No, I was~"

"Good! Great. She mentioned that you were available for anyone to use, but I wasn't sure if she got first dibs or... or whatever." He furrowed his brow and reached into his pocket for a card. "Eric Wiseman. We've met a few times."

Ari took the card. "Sure. I remember." He seemed vaguely familiar from the boardroom, but he also looked generic enough that she might be confusing him with anyone else.

"Really?" he said. "You do?"

"No. Sorry."

"Oh. Well, I have a client who may be interested in your services. Background checks and digging around for skeletons in the closet. You do that, right?"

Ari nodded. "I do."

"Excellent. I'll be in touch with more details." He extended his hand before realizing she was holding a coffee cup. "Oh. It's nice to, uh, officially meet you."

"Sure," she said. "Talk to you soon."

She left him and went out to the main lobby. Shannon glanced up and raised an eyebrow when Ari put the coffee cup down in front of her.

"For making your life a little tougher. I imagine the bosses around here drink stuff a little better than what they provide for you."

Shannon picked up the coffee and sniffed. "A little milk and a little sugar. How'd you know?"

"I have a sixth sense for that sort of thing." It was actually one of her main senses, the sense of smell enhanced by her *canidae* side. She knew what brands of deodorant and perfume each of the receptionists wore, along with other more personal information, just from inhaling near them. She usually tried to blind herself to those things, but every now and then it came in handy.

"I'll try to be less rude next time," Ari said.

Shannon sipped the coffee. Her eyes widened. "Wow. Bring me more of these and you can be rude whenever you want."

Ari chuckled and went to the elevators. She supposed having top-level security for the office wasn't the worst thing in the world. It would benefit all of her clients, not just those she got through GG&M. Her real complaint was with the violation of her personal space. If Cecily Parrish hadn't gotten the message that some things were out-of-bounds, Ari would just have to make sure the lawyer's next lesson was harder to ignore.

Chapter Two

ARI AND Dale often showered together due to necessity; they lived in the basement of a college student named Neka Teller, and between her and her boyfriend, the hot water never lasted very long. Doubling up was the best way to ensure neither of them had to suffer a cold shower. Then again, just because it was practical didn't mean Ari was strictly professional about it. Sex in the shower stall was unworkable but she could still appreciate her girlfriend's body as she massaged the shampoo into her scalp.

Dale closed her eyes and leaned back against Ari. "I'm thinking of cutting my hair."

"Yeah? How short?"

Dale reached up and drew a line along the base of her skull. "Around there. Maybe keep it a little longer on the side to cover up the scar."

As always when the wound was mentioned, Ari bent down and kissed the spot where Dale had been shot in the head. There had been a few terrifying moments when Ari thought the wound was fatal. The gun went off. Blood flew, and she could smell the copper in the air as Dale slumped to one side. She still sometimes saw it slowed down in her dreams. Dale's limp body collapsing into the bushes, blood on the side of her face. Even though she did get back up, Ari never wanted to forget just how lucky they'd gotten.

She focused on the present and pictured Dale with shorter hair. "I think you would look cute."

Dale pulled the hair over her shoulder. "Butch?"

"No, you're too adorable to be butch. Pixie, maybe."

Dale said, "Pixie's not too bad. Besides, if it's short, it'll cut down on how long I have to spend washing it."

Ari smiled. "Babe, out of the entire day, this is not the chore I want to shave time from."

Dale grinned over her shoulder. "Oh, yeah? You like it, huh?"

"It's good." Ari smoothed the hair over Dale's shoulders and down her back. She rested her hands on Dale's hips and Dale responded by pressing back tighter against her. Ari slipped her hands around to Dale's belly.

"What are you doing, puppy?" Dale whispered, her voice barely audible over the spray.

"Hm? Nothing. Take down the showerhead."

Dale took it down and ran the spray over her breasts, letting the water wash over her stomach before it was dammed by Ari's hands. Ari kissed Dale's neck.

"Short hair would make that better, too," Dale pointed out.

Ari said, "How so?"

"It wouldn't get in my eyes when I'm looking down at you."

"Mm, then I'm sold."

Ari's hand to the matted red hair of Dale's mound. Sex in the shower wasn't feasible. But everyone masturbated in the shower from time to time, and all Ari was doing was providing a helping hand. She extended two fingers between Dale's thighs and stroked her. Dale aimed the water so it washed over Ari's hands, wetting Ari's fingers and trickling down her thighs. She reached back with her other hand, but Ari intercepted it.

"Nope... hand on the soap dish. We don't want you to fall again."

The porcelain dish was built into the wall and had a short grab-bar on the top. Dale wrapped her fingers around it and bowed her head as Ari continued to tease her. Ari kissed across Dale's shoulders and pulled her closer, feeling every tremble in Dale's body as she neared orgasm. She nipped her earlobe and whispered Dale's name as her middle finger parted the lips and began slowly thrusting.

"Two," Dale said.

Ari added a second finger and moved her hand to Dale's breast.

She brushed her thumb over the nipple as Dale tensed and rolled her head back. Her breath came in short gasps before she turned her head. Ari found her lips and kissed her. After a few final tremors Dale twisted in Ari's embrace to kiss her properly. She kept the showerhead in her hand, the water washing over Ari's ass.

"Your turn," Ari said.

"Do I have to do it in the shower?"

"Well, I'd hate to stifle your creativity."

Dale kissed her again. She dragged one finger down Ari's chest, breaking their eye contact to watch as the beads of water were smeared by its passage. "Finish up in here. Take your time drying off. I'll meet you in the bedroom."

She stretched to hang the showerhead back up. Ari took the chance to admire Dale's body, patted her hip as she left the stall, and moved under the spray. She washed her hair and turned off the water just after it turned cold. She dried off but left her hair smoothed down and dripping as she went out into the bedroom. Dale was sitting on their bed in a V-neck T-shirt with a pillow over her lap.

"You know, if I had my hair cut short, we could do all kinds of roleplay."

"Yeah? Like what?"

Dale moved the pillow to reveal she was wearing the strap-on. "You know how you always wanted to be Sandy in *Grease?*"

"That's not a fantasy I ever recall having," Ari said as she moved closer to the bed. "Besides, you'd need a leather jacket for that, stud."

"So it's a work in progress. C'mere."

Ari straddled Dale's lap and sank down, letting the toy bump against her thighs as she bent down for a kiss. She reached between them and moved the tip so she could sink down onto it. Dale put one hand on Ari's thigh, the other in the small of her back, and bit her lip as Ari settled on top of her. Ari wrapped her arms around Dale's shoulders and began to move against the dildo in a slow rhythm. She kept her eyes locked on Dale's face until she sensed the attention and looked up.

"What are you doing, puppy?"

"Looking at you."

"Oh?" She kissed Ari's breasts. "Like what you see?"

Ari moved her hands up into Dale's hair. "Mm, very much. You?"

"I wish you were wearing your collar... but otherwise... very nice."

Soon the threat of a cramp in Ari's right leg forced them to change positions, with Ari lying on her stomach underneath Dale. They finished quickly after that, Ari hugging the pillow as Dale thrust into her from behind. Afterward Dale collapsed on top of her, kissing her face through the hair that had fallen over it like a shroud. They stayed like that for a moment before Dale withdrew the strap-on. Ari gasped as it brushed against hypersensitive flesh and Dale whispered an apology.

"S'okay..."

Dale took the condom off the dildo and tossed it in the trash. When she twisted to take off the harness, Ari reached up and did it for her.

"Thank you, puppy."

"Sure." She smoothed her hand over the red marks the strap had left on Dale's hip. She put the toy away, slipped on a pair of boyshorts, and rejoined Ari in bed. She spooned her from behind and kissed her shoulder. "No run tonight?"

"Not tonight."

"Okay. Night."

It didn't take long for Dale's breathing to become steady and slow, but Ari kept finding distractions that kept her from falling asleep. They'd spent the day learning the new security features in the office so neither of them would accidentally set it off. A sudden burst of paranoia had led her to ask Fogerson if there was any way Cecily could use the new tech to spy on them.

"You mean like a back door?" Fogerson had asked, looking genuinely confused.

"Something like that, yeah."

He said, "Even if there was a way to do that, I wouldn't include it. It would be unethical."

She had apologized for the insinuation, but her mind wasn't entirely at ease. Now, hours later, she was still thinking about it. Cecily was in charge of putting the cameras in, so she might have included something that wasn't disclosed. She rolled over and stared at the ceiling. Dale's hand slid over her stomach and the fingers curled into a loose fist. Ari stroked Dale's arm and stared at the ceiling. She could hear movement above them in the main house, Neka moving through the kitchen or dining room. Her mind began to wander, so she let it move through various subjects until it landed on the thing that was keeping her up.

It didn't take long. She kept thinking back to Cecily Parrish's offer. When her probation ran out, she was going to be presented with a choice. A regular paycheck, an office at GG&M, and regular casework. It felt like selling out, giving up everything she'd built from scratch in exchange for something easy. How was that different from taking money from her mother? Then again, it was technically a lateral move. She would still be a private investigator, a job she loved, so what did it matter if she had a boss? She liked being her own boss. She was proud of what she and Dale had turned Bitches into over the years. But lots of people worked for someone. It didn't mean they had given up.

But the money... the money, the money. No more worrying about the rent or praying the sound coming out of the car's engine would go away on its own. Becoming GG&M's in-house investigator equaled peace of mind. They could build up their savings and still afford to move into a house or an apartment. Something more worthy than some college student's basement. Dale had found their current home perfect because it was like a wolf's den; it was underground, it was like a cave, it was perfect for the wolf side of Ari's personality. But was it perfect for a redheaded Human from Pennsylvania? Dale deserved a yard, a picket fence, a view of the water. She deserved something better than living in a literal hole in the ground.

As if sensing Ari's thoughts, Dale snuggled closer to her. Ari stroked her back and held her, letting Dale's head find a comfortable place on her shoulder. She didn't have to make a decision that night, and she probably wouldn't be asked to until after her probationary period ended. She could talk it over with Dale, who would be most affected by whatever road she chose.

It was very hard to imagine a job where Dale wasn't her partner and Bitches wasn't in her life, but she had to figure out if that sentimentality was going to end up holding them back.

Eric Wiseman called the next morning not long after Ari and Dale arrived at the office. They mutually decided to skip the morning jog so they could go a little - okay, extraordinarily - out of their way for breakfast tacos from Chinook's. It was raining, so on the way back Dale drove them past the sidewalk where a website called Rainworks had left a piece of invisible art. The image - Peter Pan flying over the motto 'Never Grow Up' - was only visible when it was wet, and similar surprise illustrations had been popping up all over Seattle the past few months.

Back at the office, they had just set everything up to eat together at Dale's desk when the phone rang. Dale washed down her first bite of taco with a sip of milk before she answered.

"Bitches Investigations, how may we help you? One moment please." She put the receiver against her shoulder. "Eric Wiseman from GG&M."

"Thank you, Miss Frye. I'll take it in the office."

Dale batted her eyelashes and asked Eric to hold for a moment. Ari took her food into the main office and stepped around her desk. The line was flashing as she took a seat.

"This is Ari."

"Hello, Miss Willow. Eric Wiseman. We spoke yesterday."

"I remember." She picked up a piece of bacon that had fallen from her taco and popped it into her mouth. "Did you discuss my involvement with your client?"

"I did, and they agreed to bring you in. You may be aware that Seattle is finally getting a hockey team. The Totems. They're scheduled to make a grand debut this summer before joining the league in October. They were recruiting players while the ink on the deal was still wet, but they're keeping the names quiet until the whole team is officially signed. They want to reveal themselves as a complete entity, you know, not some patchwork creation."

Ari took a bite of her taco; it was clear Eric didn't plan to let her talk for a while.

"So it'll be a grand unveiling of the Seattle Totems for the entire world to see. But here's the problem. The team is plucking up these guys from all over the place. We've got Swedes, Russians, a Czech. But the majority of the guys are coming from Washington. You know, homegrown athletes. Get the crowd behind them right away. The owners are interested in making sure they're picking the right lineup. They want players who will not only lead the team to victory, but will represent the city of Seattle in a good light in the media. You know Kevin Durant?"

"Basketball player."

"Right. Great basketball player, but off the court, he's a genuine guy who loves his mother and plays pick-up games with local kids. The team doesn't need anyone to be perfect, just someone the people will want to support."

Ari said, "You want me to look into them, see if there are any skeletons in the closet."

"Exactly. Criminal records, too many traffic tickets, six kids in six different states, anything that would look bad on the front page of the Sports section. I'll send you a copy of what we have. Players names, where they're from, what the team has managed to figure out on their own. It should be a jumping off point, at least."

"Am I allowed to talk with the team directly?"

"Absolutely. Set it up with me, I'll talk to the team owner, they'll~"

Ari said, "Those are a lot of go-betweens. I'd rather be able to contact the players directly if I have any questions."

Wiseman hesitated. "Okay. Yes, of course, that makes sense. I'll include their contact information in the email. But the owner would like you to be as discreet as possible. If word gets out that you're investigating them, they might start covering stuff up."

"That makes sense. What's the timeline on this?" Ari asked. "I figure there are quite a few players on the team, and digging into all of them will take a while."

"The press conference to reveal the roster is scheduled for three months from now. If you find anything that requires a player to be substituted, the team will need time to find someone. Would six weeks be reasonable?"

"For how many players? I'm not a hockey girl."

"Twenty."

Ari said, "Yeah, that's doable. I'll keep you updated as I go. If I find something damning tomorrow, your client will have the whole three months to find a replacement."

"Fantastic. I just hit send on the packet."

Ari turned and tapped her keyboard to wake the computer up. The screen flickered to life and she logged in, clicked to her email, and found the message.

"There it is, safe and sound."

"Do we need to discuss your compensation?"

"Cecily deals with that. I'm paid to be available whenever someone needs me and, now that you need me, I'm earning my paycheck."

Eric said, "Okay, then. We'll be in touch, Miss Willow."

"Ari. If we're going to be talking a lot, I don't want to feel like I'm talking to my principal."

He chuckled. "Fair enough. Anything else?"

"I think that'll take care of it."

"Good luck, Mi... Ari. Although I guess I should say bad luck since I'm hoping you don't find anything damning."

Ari smiled. "I get paid either way, so maybe you should just wish I don't get too bored."

"Done."

She said goodbye and hung up. She opened the file and skimmed the list of names, none of which meant much of anything to her. There might be people all over Seattle willing to give their left hand to see these names. She glanced toward the ceiling as if she could see evidence of the security system Cecily had installed the day before. Maybe she had a point about beefing up their protection. She didn't think anyone would actually break in to read a roster, but it was nice knowing the information was safe.

Ari made a copy of the list and saved it to her phone. She would get Dale to help her out with some of the computer stuff, since she was so much better at scouring the internet and building profiles of people. If they split the work, she could spare the time to give everyone a thorough investigation and still turn in a final report well before the deadline. She'd start on the first name immediately.

Just as soon as she finished her breakfast taco.

CHAPTER THREE

"YOU HAVE the roster of the Seattle Totems on your computer as we speak?"

Ari was taken aback by Dale's enthusiasm. She was sitting on the edge of Dale's desk to fill her in about the conversation with Wiseman, but as soon as the team was brought up, Dale reached out and grabbed her arm.

"I didn't know you cared so much about hockey. I've literally never heard you mention it."

"No, I probably haven't. But my Dad loves it. When I was a kid, he was at work all the time. But the three hours a hockey game was on, I knew he would be in the living room in his recliner. So that was where I would be. It didn't even matter if I didn't have his whole attention. He asked me about school and my friends and everything over the commercial breaks. So no, I don't like hockey. I like the commercial breaks." She smiled. "Dad's extremely excited that Seattle's getting a team. He mentions it in all of his emails. I guess I'm mostly excited on his behalf."

Ari leaned over the desk to kiss the top of Dale's head. "You're adorable. Do you want me to keep the list to myself so you won't be tempted to tell him anything?"

"No, I think I can restrain myself. I'd hate to make you do all that work on your own."

"Because it's a lot of work?"

"Because I'm better at it."

Ari gasped in fake offense. "How dare you. I taught you everything you know."

"And then I re-trained myself to do it right."

"We're fighting now."

"Okay, sweetie."

Ari grinned and went back into her office. "The roster's in your email. Look it over, see if anything jumps out at you. Do we have anything going on right now?" The agreement with GG&M was that anything they brought to Ari became her top priority, but she didn't want to just ignore other paying clients just because something else came along.

"We're in a lull. We do have that surveillance thing for Dickerson, but that's only Sunday nights. You can do both, right?"

"Yeah. Research by day, stalking by night." She finished logging out of her computer and let the screen go black before she returned to Dale's desk. "So, what do you think?"

Dale was scanning the screen. "Anticlimactic. I don't recognize any of these names. But looking it over, a handful of them live in Canada so it will take some time and effort to get into their files. We'll put them off for a while. One of them lives in Chicago. One of them is in Boston. But a good chunk of them either live right here in Seattle or nearby."

"Wiseman said that was a big draw. Root, root, root for the home team, you know." She put her hands on the edge of the desk and leaned over so she could see the screen. "I'm leaving it up to you, Dale. Who should be our first victim?"

Joseph Levesque lived in a boxy condo in Whittier Heights, a non-descript residence notable mainly for its ugly red-orange paint job. They decided to start from the middle out rather than taking the list alphabetically. It made as much sense as any other angle, since they had nothing to go on for any of the names. Ari parked at the corner with her tablet propped against the steering wheel. Dale had already found enough information about Levesque for a short bio. Ari propped her phone up on the dashboard and put it on speaker.

"Levesque is a center coming in from the Quebec League. That's junior hockey."

"How old is he?"

"Nineteen."

Ari whistled. "That's worse than the NBA. At least those kids usually go to college first."

"Sure, but these kids are living their dreams. And Levesque's been dreaming about this since he was a kid. Mite, Squirt, Peewee, Bantam, Midget..."

Ari frowned at the phone. "Why are you saying these words?"

"They're amateur ice hockey leagues. It means Levesque's been playing since he was... let's see... six years old. His whole life, basically."

Ari did the math in his head. "That's only thirteen years. Thirteen years ago, I was... shit, I was older than he is now. We're old, Dale."

"You'll always be older than me, puppy."

Ari sighed. "Okay, so he's Canadian?"

"French Canadian. He lived in Quebec until he was fifteen, so we'll have to dig around up there if we want to find out what he was up to before coming here."

"In the meantime, we can find out if he's living clean in the States."

"I don't know what to expect," Dale said. "On the one hand, these are all pretty young kids from what I've seen. There's one guy who is twenty-eight. Oh, here are some guys in their thirties. They must be the old guard. Anyway, the young bucks haven't had much chance to get in trouble."

Ari said, "Yeah, these squeaky-clean teenagers and kids in their twenties. Real pillars of society. Especially the athletes."

Dale laughed. "Okay, you have a point, I guess."

Halfway down the block, the garage door of Levesque's house began to rise. "Hold on, he's leaving. I may have to follow him."

"High-speed chase through the streets of Seattle."

"More likely a low crawl through the side streets of Ballard while a kid who can't even drink yet goes about his errands."

Levesque was a slender young black man in a skintight shirt and skinny jeans. He wheeled a motorcycle out onto the driveway and disappeared back into the garage. When he returned, he was carrying a bucket with a bag of cleaning supplies over his shoulder.

"Oh, geez, it's worse than I thought," Ari said. "I have to watch a guy wash his bike."

"Is he at least shirtless?"

"Doesn't look like he's going that way."

Dale clucked her tongue. "Be brave."

Ari grinned. "See what you can find on the other guys. I'll call you back later."

"Love you."

"I love you, too."

Ari disconnected the call and moved the phone to the charger. She took a baseball cap off the passenger seat and pulled it low over her eyes. If anyone questioned what she was doing, she could say that she'd gotten tired while driving and chose to pull over instead of continuing on. As Levesque began washing his bike, Ari feared she might not have to feign exhaustion if things didn't pick up soon.

Nicole Vasquez worked at a coffee shop near the Space Needle. According to the Facebook status Dale found, her shift ended at five-thirty. Ari was waiting outside at a quarter past. While she watched Joseph Levesque wash his motorcycle, Dale had been doing a deep dive on another player. Brett Potter was a lifelong Seattleite, a twenty-two-year-old former honor student currently enrolled at U-Dub. Dale didn't find any record of a scholarship, but his social media was awash with pictures of him in various hockey uniforms.

His Facebook also revealed he'd recently broken up with his girlfriend of three years. Six minutes after her shift ended, Nicole came outside with a bag dangling from one arm and a phone clutched in her other hand. Ari got out of her car and moved on an intercept course, smiling when Nicole realized this stranger was approaching her.

"Can I help you?"

"Hi. My name is Ariadne Willow. I'm a private investigator."

Both eyebrows flicked upward at that. "Really?" She put the phone back to her ear. "Aspen, I have to go. There's a private investigator who wants to talk to me. Seriously." She hung up and then held the phone out in front of her. "Can I take your picture?"

"Uh." The flash blinked. "Sure. I guess."

"What's up? What did I do?"

Ari said, "Nothing that I know of. I've been hired to perform background checks for a certain company's future employees. Do you know a Brett Potter?"

Nicole laughed and crossed her arms over her chest. "Brett's actually going to get a job? I'll believe that when I see it. What even is he qualified for?"

"I'm afraid I can't reveal that. They're just interested in getting a character reference."

"Okay." She looked toward the street, her lips pursed in thought. "Brett's actually an okay guy. He's nice, he's sweet, he means well. But he's got a one-track mind and that track doesn't have anything to do with being responsible. For anything. You think he's gonna hold down a nine-to-five job? Good luck. The only thing he gives a damn about is hockey."

Ari tried to look surprised. "He's an athlete?"

"Whoever hired you didn't tell you that? Because Brett sure as shit brought it up in his job interview. Hell, he probably wore a jersey to the office. Long story short, Brett's not a bad dude. If I could have counted on him a bit more, we'd probably still be dating. But you're never going to get his brain off the ice. I'll guarantee you that."

"Okay. Thank you, that's very helpful. Thank you for your time."

Nicole hesitated. "This is really for a job, right? You're not just saying that?"

"No, someone definitely wants to hire him. Why?"

"It's just easier to believe he's in trouble than he might actually make something of himself. He spends every waking hour in skates. Or playing video games based on hockey. Can you imagine being so completely obsessed with something?"

Ari shook her head. "It's surprising. But I promise you, Brett's not in trouble."

"Good. Cool. Thanks."

"Sure. Have a nice afternoon."

Ari walked back to her car and opened her tablet to fill in what she'd learned about Brett. So far she'd been bored by one potential player doing chores and heard that another might end up being the most dedicated player in the NHL. She told herself to appreciate the dullness while it lasted, because sooner or later she was going to find the black sheep on the roster.

On Sunday, Ari watched Oscar Lindeman drive two women she assumed were his mother and grandmother to church. He didn't go in with them, but he sat in the car and read a book for two hours until they came back out. Ari watched him the entire time from a parking lot across the street just to make sure wasn't using the occasion to meet with any drug dealers or crime lords. While she surveilled him, she read Dale's latest update. She'd found a few players with police records. That perked Ari's interest until she discovered it was all teenage misdemeanor crap; graffiti, loitering, skateboarding. Lindeman and his family headed for lunch at a nearby restaurant. Ari took the chance he wouldn't get up to any mischief and went off to check out the next name on her list.

Sunday night she put a hold on the team's investigation so she could work her surveillance gig. Her case took her to the moorage at a marina on Lake Union where several boats had been vandalized over the past few weeks. The vandals only struck on Sunday, so there was no point in staking it out the rest of the week.

She parked at the end of the lot, where pavement gave way to a thin strip of grass and then water that looked black as ink. The Space Needle was beautifully shining to the southwest, like a small UFO hovering between her and the lights of downtown. The day had been hot so she rolled down the window to let the cooler night breezes push out the stale warmer air out of the car. She was parked so she could see the entrance as well as most of the berths and settled in for a long night of waiting. A laptop screen would have given off far too much light, so she'd asked Dale to print off a few bios of Totems players. She used a small flashlight that could be easily concealed and spent the long night reading about what had to be the most squeaky-clean group of athletes she'd ever come across.

Some of the players had parking tickets, speeding tickets, minor offenses that all law-abiding citizens acquired in the course of owning a car. A few other players had been caught with a DUI or two, but there were no rehabs or secret families waiting to be uncovered. The moorage also remained unmolested, without a sign of anybody trespassing or marking the boats. At one point she got out of the car to stretch her legs and to make sure no one was casing the marina before striking. Just south of the marina, a row of houseboats stretched out onto the lake, and she counted time by when the residents turned out their lights to go to bed.

At dawn she walked along the docks just to make sure no one had somehow managed to vandalize the boats without being seen, but everything looked to be in order. She left a report for the owner, dragged herself home, and crawled into bed just as Dale was getting out of the shower.

They cuddled as Ari reported what she'd uncovered, one on the verge of unconsciousness while the other was struggling to wake up.

"Isn't it good that none of them are monsters, though?" Dale asked. "It means the Totems are going to be a team Seattle can proudly support."

"I guess in the grand scheme, yes. But if I go back to Cecily empty-handed, I'm afraid it's going to look like I just didn't dig deep enough." She closed her eyes. "Lack of results implies lack of effort."

"Or maybe it proves lack of evidence," Dale whispered. "We're just getting started. You're scratching the surface. If there's something to find... puppy? Ariadne? Are you asleep?"

"Mm."

Dale leaned in and kissed Ari's lips. "Go to sleep, puppy. You'll get 'em next week."

Ari's features were already slack with sleep, so Dale eased her way out of bed and tiptoed out of the room.

CHAPTER FOUR

AARON RIGBY was a promising candidate for shenanigans. He was one of the team elders at thirty-one. Already twice divorced, Dale discovered his credit card was frequently used at bars in the wee hours of the morning. It took time to track down his most recent ex-wife, a hotel receptionist, but Ari was finally able to sit down with her on Wednesday morning. It turned out he would wait in the hotel bar until she finished her shift, buying coffees to keep himself awake so he could drive her home at the end of her shift. Not just a good guy, a contender for Husband of the Year Award.

She was beginning to get seriously disillusioned with the case. She spoke to ex-girlfriends, former bosses, neighbors, and friends. Dale tracked down old team rosters and Ari interviewed old teammates.

"Great guy," one said, unable or unwilling to elaborate. "Gladstone's just, I don't know, Gladstone. He's a good guy. We'd grab a beer sometimes."

Another looked confused by the concept. "Faults? I don't know. He can be a little moody. Who isn't sometimes, though."

One girlfriend had asked, a little too enthusiastically, "He's not dead, is he?"

The closest she came to a lead was Chuck Weaver's former high school coach who cut him from the team over drugs. He was caught with some marijuana and the school had a zero tolerance policy.

By Friday night she'd done a pretty thorough job looking into seven of the prospective players and hadn't found anything that would make a sports website salivate for an exclusive. Ari typed up background information on each one that would've put Wikipedia to shame, then leaned back and stared at the screen. She rocked her chair back and forth as she looked at the results of the past few days, frustrated at how little there was.

Dale knocked on the open door. "Hey, puppy. How's it going?"

Ari slumped forward.

"Yeah. I kind of got that impression." She came into the office and opened the bureau where Ari kept a spare change of clothes. A dry-cleaner bag she didn't remember putting there was hanging among the T-shirts, and Dale took it out. "This is your red blouse. Those black slacks you like are in there, too. You're going to change into them, and I'm going to change into that green dress, and we're going out to dinner at McCormick's."

"McCormick's?" Ari sat up straighter. "You need a reservation to get... you got a reservation."

Dale shrugged. "When you got this case, I knew it would be a lot of chasing your tail, reading files, and not a lot of interesting or exciting developments. I figured you would need a date night to take your mind off of it."

Ari stood up and leaned across the desk. She cupped Dale's face and kissed her. "You are objectively the best girlfriend in the world."

"I know. Hurry up and change. We should get there early."

Ari eagerly saved her work and shut down her computer. Her mood instantly lifted just at the thought of spending a romantic evening with her partner. She changed and escorted Dale out the door, leaving the case for the next day.

The restaurant was on Columbia and Fourth. It was cheaper to park a few blocks away and walk the difference, so they linked arms and strolled downhill toward the restaurant. They passed someone selling flowers and Ari bought a rose for Dale, who tucked it behind her ear after confirming there weren't any uncut thorns.

When they arrived, the hostess looked at Ari's collar before leading them to a table. Ari was used to the sideways glances. The collar was a simple strip of leather with a gold clasp. There weren't studs or elaborate chrome fasteners that would indicate a BDSM connection. It was their version of a promise ring, a testament to her commitment to their relationship. Dale had a bracelet of Ari's hair woven together with a lock of fur from the wolf, and Ari looked at it as they took a seat. Dale caught her looking and twisted her wrist in acknowledgement.

The rule was no talk about hockey or the players during dinner. The Totems had taken full command of Ari's mind for the past week and she needed something to cleanse her mental palate. They talked about Ari's mother and Dale's father. Dale mentioned she'd gotten a few emails from Milo and the British pack. She watched Ari throughout their conversation and the meal, noticing how the tension seemed to evaporate from her in ever-increasing increments until she was sitting up straight and actually smiling.

Ari took Dale's hand as they left the restaurant. "That was exactly what the doctor ordered." She kissed Dale's cheek. "Thank you, sweetie."

Dale smiled. "Anything to help you relax. I'm just glad it worked."

They turned left out of the restaurant and, as they walked, Dale noticed several things that she didn't fully connect until much later. A truck slowed down as it passed them, but there was an intersection coming up. It was apparently there, under the currently red light, where the truck pulled a highly illegal U-turn, sped up crossing the wrong way across four lanes of traffic. The engine rose to a low growl as it closed the distance. Traffic was light, but a chorus of horns and shrieking tires still erupted to life in response.

None of these things registered to Dale consciously in the moment, but her subconscious put them together. The flash of lights was enough to trigger something primal in the back of her mind, a survival instinct that told her they were in danger. It was just enough of a warning for her to turn around in time to see the truck bearing down on them. Its headlights were off as it clambered up onto the curb. A line of trees prevented the truck from fully climbing onto the sidewalk, a fact that may have saved their lives.

"Puppy!" Dale wrapped her arms around Ari's waist and hurled them both closer to the buildings. Ari instinctively put her arms around Dale and turned them as they fell so that she would land on the ground and cushion Dale's landing. They cleared its path with inches to spare. Dale's foot twisted off the pavement and swung up to be tapped by the bumper as it passed. They hit the sidewalk hard, knocking the wind from both of them. Traffic was frozen, and a group of pedestrians were forming a circle around where Ari and

Dale had fallen. A few people were advancing on the truck with their phones extended to take pictures of the driver, even though the windshield was obviously tinted.

"Maniac!" someone shouted. Another person rushed forward to see if Ari and Dale were okay.

The truck reversed as quickly as it had accelerated, tires spinning on the sidewalk before finding purchase. Someone was talking to 911 on their cell phone, and now people were coming out of the restaurant to see what had just happened.

Ari touched Dale's face and shoulders. Her eyes were wide with panic, the irises shrunken by the surge of adrenaline. "Are you okay?"

"I'm fine." Dale could almost feel the wolf trembling under Ari's skin. Her ankle was throbbing with an injury she couldn't feel yet the pain from. "Go. Go!"

Ari got up and started running after the truck. Dale stood as well, crying out when she put weight on her left foot. The truck reached the intersection, spun around, and drove in the right direction down the steep hill of Columbia.

"Wait, 911 is on the way," someone told her.

"We need to get the license plate!" Dale shouted without slowing. Her foot was definitely messed up, but she limped on. Ari had a huge lead on her and ran into the dark open mouth of the parking garage across from McCormick's. Dale followed her, already well aware of what Ari's plan was. She ran into the garage as well and stooped to pick up Ari's shoes. Next she found her slacks with the panties still tangled inside of them, then the jacket and blouse lying right by the Columbia Street exit. The shoulder of the jacket was ripped, but it had spared the blouse from the same fate. Ari would be happy to see one of her favorite blouses was unmarred.

Dale bundled the clothes under her left arm as she stood in the entrance and looked down toward the water. There was no sign of the truck or Ari. She leaned against the concrete wall and finally risked looking down at her left foot. No blood, no obvious disfigurement, but it was throbbing like it was about to fall off. Running probably hadn't been a good idea, but she knew Ari's intention had been to transform. She didn't want to leave the trail of discarded clothes behind for just anyone to discover.

Now, though, she had to deal with the police. She opened her purse and found a way to fit all of Ari's clothes into it.

"Go get the son of a bastard, puppy," she whispered. She turned and used the wall to keep the weight off her foot as she limped back toward the scene of the crime.

Ari dropped to all fours while she was still mostly human, her palms slapping twice against the pavement before twisting into paws. She didn't even consider the few seconds she spent completely naked in the parking garage but she was vaguely aware that she didn't see any headlights or shouts of surprise when she stripped out of her clothes and began transforming, so she assumed she'd gotten away without being spotted. She followed the slope of the ground to the exit and emerged with the truck still in sight. It swept through the next intersection without even touching its brakes, causing another blast of horns and screeching brakes.

Ears flat, Ari raced downhill in pursuit as the truck took a hard left onto Second. She caught up quickly due to the wolf's speed and the fact the truck was slowed by weaving in and out of traffic in an attempt to get away. Ari could hear sirens rising up throughout the city but she was only focused on the truck. Her wolf brain filled with base, primal thoughts: anger, fear, pain. Her entire back and right arm hurt from hitting the pavement. Dale had kneed her in the side when they fell, a minor ailment considering the pain she'd seen on Dale's face before taking off.

Whoever was in the truck had hurt them, hurt *Dale*. The wolf was determined to make them pay.

Ari reached Second Street in time to see the truck make a right turn onto James. She put her head down and slammed into a pedestrian's legs as she continued her pursuit. The pain in her legs didn't matter. The throbbing in her spine was just a reminder that she'd be sore in the morning. All that mattered was the black GMC truck.

At the corner she realized the truck hadn't turned onto James Street at all; it had pulled into the Sinking Ship parking garage. She ran in as well, slowing to a trot to examine the cars on both sides of the aisle. She finally spotted it on the other side of the structure, the engine still ticking as it cooled. No sign of the driver, but she dropped her head and sniffed the ground near the driver's side door. Dozens, hundreds of comingled scents, body odor and shoe leather and perfumes, but one was distinctly recent.

She followed it to the edge of the asphalt and peered over the edge. The Sinking Ship was actually the last remnant of the Seattle Hotel, rising from a triangular crossing of streets with made it look like a sailing ship lost to the waves. The drop to the pavement from this particular spot was over ten feet. It would hurt, but it was doable for someone with the right motivation.

Ari scanned the sparse crowd for signs of anyone moving with a limp. No one jumped out at her so she left the garage and moved to the sidewalk. She put her snout to the ground again and tried to pick up the driver's scent. Pedestrians gave her a wide berth, while some took out their phones to take pictures of her. She was sure Instagram and Twitter would be full of people spotting the #SeattleWolf, but she didn't care about that. There were too many people, too many scents to pick up one in particular. From where she was, the driver could've gone down Occidental, Yesler, Second Avenue, into or between any of the buildings nearby. He could be blocks away before she got the scent back.

"He's wearing a collar," a woman said, "see if he has a tag."

Ari pulled away just before the well-meaning woman's companion got his hand on her collar. He withdrew his hand but Ari knew he wouldn't give up easily. Other pedestrians were starting to gather to help the poor lost dog, so she knew her options were to abandon the chase or risk spending the night in a kennel. She turned and sprinted between her would-be savior and his female companion. She didn't stop until she was back where the chase had started.

Police cars were lined up at the curb in front of the parking garage, their lights casting silhouettes in red and blue against the surrounding buildings. An ambulance was sitting near where the truck had jumped the curb and Dale was sitting in the back. Two uniformed officers were flanking her while an EMT examined her left foot.

Dale looked past them and spotted Ari. She pressed her lips together and dipped her chin. Ari nodded back to her. It killed her to leave Dale behind but there wasn't much else she could do. She couldn't exactly approach Dale to get her clothes back, so she crossed the street and continued on toward home. It was a mile and a half run, barely worth noticing for the wolf even after chasing the truck.

When she arrived, she slipped into the backyard and transformed to get out the hide-a-key and let herself inside. Dale had left her phone when they went out to dinner. Ari put on a T-shirt and some sweatpants before she called the police on their non-emergency tip line.

"Seattle Police, how can I help you?"

"My name is Ariadne Willow. I'm a private investigator and I was involved in a near hit-and-run earlier tonight at the corner of Columbia and Fourth. Vehicle was a late model GMC, black." She closed her eyes and recited the license plate number before it faded from her memory due to transforming out of the wolf form. "I pursued the vehicle on foot to where it was abandoned at the Sinking Ship parking garage on Second."

"You pursued it on foot?"

"It nearly ran over me and my girlfriend. I was motivated. The truck should still be there if you get a car on-site as soon as possible."

"We're going to need an official statement."

"I'll be happy to give one. Later. For now, you're going to want to get that truck."

She hung up and began pacing. Fifteen minutes later, Dale limped down the stairs with a crutch under her right arm. Ari was already at the door to usher her in. They hugged tightly as soon as Dale was safely inside, clinging to one another for a long moment before Ari stepped back to look down.

"How bad is it?"

"As un-bad as it can be," Dale said. "Ankle sprain. The crutch is just because I aggravated the injury by running after you. I have all your clothes, by the way."

"Thank you," Ari muttered, distracted as she examined Dale's shoulders and elbows for signs of any injury she wasn't mentioning.

Dale gently flapped Ari's hands away. "My foot got twisted when I jumped out of the way, but I jumped at just the right angle to not go under the tire."

Ari muttered, "Another lucky angle, huh?"

"What?"

"Nothing." She cupped Dale's face. "I'm so glad you're safe. I felt your body jerk. I saw the pain on your face and I thought--"

Dale covered Ari's hand with her own. "It doesn't matter what you thought, because I'm fine."

"This time." Ari dropped her arm and stepped away. "How many lucky breaks are we going to get, Dale? Shot in the head, and the angle was just right for you to survive. You get hit by a truck and again the angle just happens to be perfect. You were standing unarmed in the street in the middle of a gunfight because of a war between *canidae* and hunters. What about next time? What if that driver had timed it so we were in the crosswalk and he mowed us down? You keep getting hurt because you just happen to be standing next to me. How many times are we going to get lucky?"

Dale looked confused and concerned. "It comes with the job."

"Well, maybe it shouldn't."

"What's that supposed to mean?"

Ari had moved closer to the kitchen, widening the gap between them. "The job Cecily Parrish offered me is still on the table. When the probationary period ends, she's going to offer me something full-time. I could be an in-house investigator for the firm."

"What about me? What about Bitches, the company you built from scratch?"

"I'd be willing to give it up if it meant you would be safe."

Dale clenched her jaw and took a deep breath before she spoke. "So you go sit in an office at GG&M and I... what, go work at McDonalds?"

"At least you would be safe there."

Dale scoffed and shook her head. "Or some psycho could come in and shoot the place up. The world is a dangerous place, Ariadne. I could get shot at any job. I would also be miserable in another job. I proved that while you were up in the mountains with your mother last summer. I just... I don't want some tedious paycheck. I want to be with you, I want to be part of the agency we built, and if that ends up being a little dangerous... then that's the price."

Ari leaned against the kitchen doorway and hung her head. "I'm not willing to sacrifice you because of choices I make."

"That's not your decision, Ariadne."

They stared each other down in silence. Finally Dale hissed and shifted her weight from the heel of her undamaged foot to the toes. "Shit."

"You should go lie down."

"Right."

She used the crutch to maneuver herself around Ari, limping toward the bedroom. She was almost there when Ari said her name without turning around.

"I know we're in a fight, and I know ordinarily I'd give you your space by sleeping on the couch, but I almost lost you tonight. I need to hold you even though you're mad at me."

Dale said, "Come on."

Ari sighed softly, relieved, and turned off the light as she followed Dale into the bedroom. They could discuss their options in the morning when they were both more level-headed. Ari would hate to just surrender Bitches Investigations and go to work for someone else. Everything Dale said had made sense, but she couldn't make herself believe it. She loved having Dale as her employee, partner, sounding board, companion. The idea of giving all that up was terrifying. But she didn't know how many times she could come this close to losing Dale before the stress become overwhelming.

Chapter Five

In the dream, Ari saw Dale hit from behind, flung forward and rolling across the pavement in a mess of blood and broken bones. She heard Dale scream as the truck hit her from the side and knocked her into traffic to be hit by another car. She saw Dale under the tires and staring with glassy eyes after the impact. Each nightmare jarred her from sleep and each time she was certain she wouldn't get back to sleep. But eventually her eyes closed and her brain gave her another horrific scenario.

She surrendered at a little past five, she gave up and got out of bed. She went into the kitchen and made tea so it would be ready when Dale woke. She wanted to call for an update about the truck but she knew it was both too early and unlikely they would share any information with her. She took out her phone and dialed Diana Macallan's number to leave a voicemail. The phone buzzed once before there was an answer.

"Hey, Ari."

She sat up straighter. "Diana. I expected the voicemail." She looked at the clock on the microwave. "What are you doing up this early? I thought you got off the zombie shift."

"Long story." Diana sounded weary. "I doubt you're just calling to shoot the breeze. What's up?"

Ari briefly detailed the night before.

"Dale was hit by a car?" Diana sounded more awake now. "Is she okay?"

"She's... yeah. She's okay. She's got a crutch for now." She rubbed her eye. "I was hoping that you could keep me updated about the truck, if they managed to find anything about the owner."

"I'll bet you dinner it was stolen. The fact it was left behind for the driver to flee on foot supports that. I'll ask around and see who is working the case."

Ari said, "Thanks, Diana. Are you okay? You sound weird. Flat."

"Calling me at five-thirty and complaining I'm not fully awake? You're a peach, Ari."

"Sorry."

"It's okay. I'm not a hundred percent, but I also don't really want to talk about it over the phone at the crack of dawn."

Ari said, "Over dinner, then? You and Lucy, me and Dale."

"Sure. We'll find a day that works for all of us."

They said their goodbyes and hung up. Ari retrieved her laptop and opened the file with the names of the Totem players. She was scrolling aimlessly through the list when Dale came out of the bedroom in shorts, a T-shirt, and her glasses instead of contacts. She was hanging off the crutch.

"Hey."

"Hey."

"You should put your weight on your hand, not-"

Dale shifted her weight. "I know."

"Sorry."

"It's okay." Dale went into the kitchen and poured herself a cup of tea. "Thank you."

"You're welcome."

Dale slowly made her way over to the table and sat down next to Ari. "Don't make decisions about my life and my job without consulting me."

"I won't. But you kind of got forced into this."

"How so?"

"You got a crash course in *canidae* when you woke up with me in your bed. And you were just going to get the agency's books in order. The job was supposed to be a few weeks, tops. Since then you've been kidnapped and shot and attacked..."

Dale smiled. "Yeah, and at no point since those first few days did I have the option to quit. Ari, I hate to tell you this, but I didn't fall in love with you at first sight."

"I'm shattered."

"I know you are. I thought you were attractive as hell. I thought you were intriguing. But I was a long way from being in love. When I was lying in a hospital with my head wrapped because some asshole shot a gun at me, don't you think it occurred to me to quit? I thought about quitting the first time we slept together because I figured it would be too weird to mix business and pleasure. There were plenty of times I could've walked out but I didn't. I loved my job before I loved you, puppy. You've overtaken it in the years since, of course."

Ari smiled and tucked her hair behind her ear.

"I'm not in danger because of you. I'm in danger because... that's the job. I'm facing it with you. We're facing it together. What about all the times you've been in danger and I saved you? Out on the island? Or when the hunters kidnapped you and dosed you with wolfsbane? Do you think that's easy for me to handle?"

"No."

"Damn right. And I want to be by your side so I can save you. Just like when I'm in danger, there's no one else I want riding to my rescue. It's you and me, puppy." She put her hand palm-up on the table and Ari put hers on top of it. "In the end, it's going to be your decision. It's a good career move. It'll probably mean a lot more money and a lot less stress due to a steady paycheck. But there are so many other factors to consider. Sleep on it. Work out the pros and cons. Please don't throw away the agency because of me."

Ari said, "I won't."

"I love you."

Ari stood up and bent down to kiss Dale's lips. "I love you, too. Now that the important stuff is out of the way... who the hell tried to run us over?"

Dale slapped her hand flat on the table. "Yeah! Who the *hell* tried to run us over?"

Ari went back to her seat and turned her computer so Dale could see the screen. "Diana said the truck is probably stolen. There might be fingerprints or some other *CSI*-type evidence, but I wouldn't count on it. If I could get access, maybe I could pick up the guy's scent."

"Or the scents of the original owner plus all the forensics people who have been crawling all over it since last night."

"Yeah." Ari rubbed her chin. "As far as suspects go, I think there are really only two options. We've got the surveillance case, and the background checks for the Totems."

Dale said, "I don't think any vandals are going to stage a hit-and-run just so they can get away with trashing a few boats."

"No, that's unlikely."

"So that leaves us with someone on the Totems."

Ari nodded. "I assume word has gotten around that I'm asking questions. Maybe someone on the team was worried I'd uncover something. I'm not sure what it could be. Everyone so far has been the perfect boy next door."

Dale said, "You've barely even scratched the surface of the people who aren't from Seattle. There are the international players to think about. I don't want to sound like a dumb American scared of foreigners, but it's a possibility."

"Yeah. Have you made any progress on getting their records?"

"The Canadians, yes. I've found a couple of resources in Vancouver and Quebec who are helping me out. Sweden is being surprisingly helpful."

Ari raised an eyebrow. "Did you find a sexy young Swiss Miss to help you out?"

"Swiss Miss is Switzerland. And no, no flirting is going on."

"Good. Are you going to work from home today?"

Dale nodded and looked down at her injured foot. "Yeah. Easier than trying to get this stupid crutch to the office. I'll be a lot more comfortable here."

"Okay, I'll go get us some breakfast. Is there anything you need from the office?"

"No, I can log in from here."

Ari stood up to kiss Dale. "My baby's got skills. I'm going to change clothes and then head out."

"Wherever you get breakfast, try to make it healthy."

"Always."

"No."

"Usually."

"Nope."

"This time I'll definitely try my best."

Dale smiled. "It's the least I can ask."

Ari chose breakfast from the Volunteer Park Cafe & Marketplace, getting the veggie quiche for Dale and a bacon and egg panini for herself. She went back home long enough to eat with

Dale before heading back out. She had a list of Totems players that she separated into those she'd already looked into and those she hadn't yet started on. The driver could've come from either column. Maybe one of the ex-girlfriends she spoke to mentioned the private investigator to her boyfriend who mentioned it to his new teammates. Nicole Vasquez took a picture of her and might have posted it to Facebook. All it would take is one of the future Totems to put two and two together to know what she was doing.

The problem now was that whoever came after them knew more than she did. He knew they were investigating Totem players so, if she turned up asking questions, he would be prepared. She'd lost the element of surprise. Letting Nicole take her picture had been dumb but there was nothing she could do about it now. She ran her eyes down the list and realized there was one person she hadn't considered. If there was a deep dark secret on the team, something so awful it would prompt an attempted homicide to keep it quiet, then the coach had to know about it.

Conor Muldoon was a former player, just famous enough for Ari to recognize his name without knowing much else about him. She looked him up and discovered he lived in Medina, a zip code so exclusive Ari felt like she'd have to rent a different car just to drive through it. She made the drive just to scope out what his place looked like and caught a lucky break: an older, grayer version of the man she'd seen on Google was getting into a Cadillac parked at the curb as she drove by.

Ari drove on to the stop sign and weighed her options. She could wait until he was gone and backtrack, transform to the wolf, and see what she could find at his house. Or, alternatively, she could take advantage of her lucky timing and follow him wherever he was going. She chose the latter and continued onward. She guessed that since Medina was mostly residential he had to be going back to Seattle. She kept an eye on her rearview mirror, watching his turn signals carefully to make sure he didn't take any unexpected turns.

"Following a suspect from the lead position," she said. "I could get used to this."

They got onto the freeway with only a few cars between them and Ari continued leading Muldoon back across Lake Washington. When he finally moved over to exit, Ari did the same thing. She pulled into the first parking lot she saw and dialed Dale's number as she waited for him to pass. The phone buzzed as she attached it to the dashboard mount so she could keep her hands free.

"Everything okay, puppy?"

"Yeah, everything's peachy." He drove past and Ari pulled back out onto the road. "I'm following the Totems coach, Conor Muldoon. I'm not sure where he's leading me, but I wanted to let you know what I was up to."

"Appreciated. I might as well give you an update. I did a quick scan of everyone's records to see if any of them had moving violations. That jackass last night pulled an illegal U-turn, drove the wrong way, and hopped the curb without any noticeable hesitation. It's got me thinking he might have done this kind of thing before. So I went through and found the names who have moving violations on their record."

"Your brain is the best brain, baby."

"Well, don't award me any points until it leads to anything. He may have just been insane enough not to worry about driving on the sidewalk. I'm going to send you the names and you can focus on those guys when you're done playing follow-the-leader."

Ari said, "Thanks. Anyone jump out at you?"

"No one in particular. A few people we've already looked into, but some we haven't."

"I'll put the new guys at the top of the list."

"Already done, puppy. Be safe."

Ari said, "You stay comfortable. Let me know if you need me to bring you anything."

"Will do. Love you."

"Love you, too."

Ari hung up and watched Muldoon's car. She put a wide gap between them in case he recognized the car he'd followed all the way from his home was still hanging around. He drove toward Lake Union and Ari smiled as they passed the marina where she was spending one night a week watching the boats.

"Muldoon is the vandal," she said, "and I'll tie up both cases in a neat little bow by catching him. That would be convenient."

Muldoon foiled her theory by continuing around the lower end of the lake and continuing back north. She sighed. If he'd been working a little harder she would think he was trying to shake her. It was more likely he was just taking a dumb route to wherever it was he was going.

After what seemed like an endless commute, he pulled into the parking lot of a glass-fronted building on the fringes of East Queen

Anne. A sign over the door identified it as Newton Ice Rink.

Ari's spirits lifted as she continued past the rink and found a place to leave her car. She walked back to give Muldoon time to get out of his car and get into the building before she showed up. The building seemed to be open to the public given the number of minivans occupying the parking lot. No one seemed to pay her any attention as she crossed to the entrance, opened the door for a party that was on their way out, and stepped inside.

The glass front of the building meant she didn't have to wait for her eyes to adjust to interior lighting. A pro shop stood to the right, along with a skate rental counter. To the left was a seating area along with four rows of small orange-fronted lockers where mothers were helping kids change from street shoes to skates. She could see the rink deeper in the building and started toward it, but a young man in a maroon polo shirt intercepted her. A tag on his chest said his name was Patrick.

"Afternoon, ma'am. Can we help you today?"

"Yeah, I'm just looking for a place to hold my niece's birthday party this weekend. I was going to do a bounce house, but apparently that's lame."

Patrick smiled. "It was cool when I was a kid."

"Me too. But I thought ice skating... might be a good fit. Is there a chance I could just take a look around? See what it's like?"

He glanced toward the counter and leaned in. "I'm not supposed to let people just wander around. And I'm really not supposed to let people in without paying the fee..."

"Five minutes?"

"Just five minutes?"

"I promise I won't go on the ice."

She was prepared to touch his arm and bat her eyelashes to get his cooperation, but he smiled and nodded his head toward the rink before she had to resort to that.

"Five minutes."

"Thanks."

She stepped around him. The entrance opened onto a wide concrete area with bleachers set up for parents to watch their kids. Ari went up into the bleachers where she could get a good look at the ice. There were mostly kids, of course, and chaperones that ranged in age from sixteen to sixty, but Ari focused on the cluster of men standing at the far end of the rink. She recognized Muldoon right away since she'd just seen him in the same clothes outside his house, but it took her a second to connect the other men with the photos she'd seen in Dale's files: Steve Aulie, Anton Oesterle, Phillipe Lindholm, and Kristof Oborin. The Totems coach and four of his players, all doing what looked like routine drills amid a gaggle of pre-teen birthday parties.

Ari couldn't imagine what they were doing at a local ice rink amid preschoolers and stay-at-home mothers. A professional hockey team must have had better places to practice. At the moment she didn't care why they were there. She only cared about the fact that she now had the chance to see a large sampling of her suspects all together and observe how they reacted. It wasn't much, but currently she was willing to take whatever she could get.

One of the players, Anton Oesterle, turned and scanned the crowd. His eyes seemed to linger on her for an unusually long time before he turned away again. Recognition? Or was he just noticing an attractive woman in the crowd? She couldn't discount either possibility. She had to operate on the possibility that any member of the team was targeting her.

As promised, Patrick came searching for her after a handful of minutes. He escorted her back toward the front of the rink.

"I hope you'll consider us for your event."

"It looks really great, Patrick. Looks like a nice place." She stopped him at the entryway. "Do you see those five guys standing at the far side of the rink? Near the bathrooms?"

Patrick looked over. "Yeah, that's Conor Muldoon and his friends. He used to be a big-time hockey player back in the day. He's in here all the time."

"With the same people?"

"Sometimes. Not always all of them together."

"What do they do?"

Patrick frowned. "What is everyone doing? They skate. They hang out. Sometimes they go to the bar. We have a bar attached, just through there. Adults only, of course."

"Right. So they've been coming here... what, for a few weeks?"

Patrick shrugged. "Something like that. I asked Mr. Muldoon for his autograph first time I saw him. Did you ever see him play? He was on the Hurricanes when I was a kid, and--"

"That's great, Patrick. Listen, I'll let my aunt know about this place."

"I thought you were the aunt..."

She was outside before he could question her further. She

didn't know if Muldoon and his quintet of players were up to anything shady, but she wasn't ready to let any of them off the hook until she knew more.

CHAPTER SIX

DALE QUICKLY discovered with a single Google search that Tyler Dubov, one of the team's defensemen, had an impressive online following. He had bounced around a couple of teams since joining the league ten years earlier, moving from Philly to Montreal to Edmonton to the other Washington, the Capitals. His role on every team seemed to be enforcer. She found a video on YouTube that compiled some of his best fights set to "Tubthumping." After the first few seconds she was cringing at every crushing impact, every blow of glove against helmet, at the spray of blood on the glass when the two brawlers finally went down.

Part of Dubov's appeal might have been the fact he was a gorgeous man under the helmet. Bright blue eyes, strong jaw, wry smile with thin sexy lips. She scrolled through a few blogs dedicated to "Dubov de Bod" that included shirtless pictures of him as well as links to sites like Gawker and Deadspin showing him out on the town. It looked like he was quite the playboy, frequently photographed outside clubs with at least two women hanging off his arms.

Her cell phone rang and she checked the screen before she answered. "Hey, Diana."

"Hi, Dale. Ari wanted me to get in touch when I found out anything on the truck, but there was no answer at the office."

"Really?" She checked the phone. "Calls should be getting forwarded here. We're working from home today, because of my ankle."

"About that. Are you okay? I know Ariadne would be more likely to exaggerate the injury instead of underselling, but I wanted to hear it from you."

Dale said, "I'm fine. Just a little sore, but nothing aspirin won't fix. Let me get a pen ready."

"There's not much to tell. The truck was stolen about an hour before you guys encountered it. Owner reported it missing from a parking lot three blocks away from Fourth. It's likely that whoever stole it was following the two of you and made a spur of the moment decision. Went out, found a truck, then came back and waited for you to come out. Maybe he was planning to follow you, staked out the place, and when you started walking the wrong way he had to make a quick decision."

Dale looked at the computer screen. She'd muted the video but it was still playing, and she watched Dubov swing around his opponent using the stick as ballast. He grabbed the other player's jersey, pulled him off his skates, and began pounding him.

"Do you know much about hockey enforcers?"

"What? No. They're the bullies, right?"

"Not really," Dale said, remembering something her father once said. "Enforcers get into a lot of fights, yes, but they're doing it as a sacrifice. They're protecting their teammates by taking the hit. They redirect aggression. They take the penalties so the more talented players can stay on the ice."

Diana said, "Uh-huh. So what's your point?"

Dale clicked back and looked at the picture of Dubov. "I'm saying if someone on a hockey team felt threatened, they wouldn't risk their own careers. They would send an enforcer."

Ari decided to call the players meeting with Muldoon at the ice rink "the Newton Five." There had to be a reason for them to meet at such an unusual location. She texted Wiseman and confirmed the team had a training facility in Tukwila. She thought maybe it was for the coach's benefit that they met here, to save him a longer drive, but she Googled the driving directions and saw it was basically the same distance. She also had a message from Dale pointing her toward Dubov and why she thought he would be worth a look.

"Beauty and brains," she said. "I really need to pay her more."

They'd received a list of every player's current address from Wiseman, and Ari saw that Dubov was conveniently staying at the Inn at Queen Anne, just over a mile away from her current location. She drove there and parked across from the ivy-coated brick building. Dubov had obviously chosen the extended-stay hotel because he'd only arrived in Seattle three weeks earlier, according to the information packet they'd gotten from GG&M. He'd been a busy boy in that time, showing up in enough paparazzi shots that most websites were ready to confirm he would be announced as a member of the Totems roster.

While she waited, she got online to check Dubov's movements over the past few weeks. Social media was a private detective's best friend. When she was training, the internet was just getting on its feet. Now with just the click of a button she could find information it would have taken ages to dig up on her own. Dubov was extremely active on Twitter, Instagram, and all the other usual suspects. Someone just going by what he posted would never guess he was a professional athlete. She scrolled through pictures of Dubov dancing at nightclubs, dancing at concerts, paddle boarding on Lake Washington. He was always surrounded by good-looking women, though Ari was pretty sure she never saw the same woman twice. It seemed he was a player in every sense of the word.

He tweeted again while she was looking at his feed. "Up & reddy 2 do it again tonite #EmeraldCity! Where u at, where shuld I go?"

Ari grimaced. "I know there are character limits, but damn, man. Learn to spell."

The replies were already coming in. People were suggesting Trinity, Re-bar, Q Nightclub, Last Supper Club, Rock Box, Alibi Room. Dubov responded to some of them to ask for more details - "Live music? Wat's the ladies like lol!" - trying to narrow down the list. When someone mentioned a karaoke bar in Capitol Hill, he jumped on it immediately.

"Can't sing, but I can KARY-OKE! I'm there! U better be their to!"

Ari grimaced. So apparently she was going to hear a barely-literate hockey enforcer sing the hits of yesteryear. She could think of worse ways to spend a night, but at the moment they all seemed preferable. She sighed and went back to checking his activity the night before. He hadn't posted anything between noon and eleven

PM, plenty of time to do a little light stalking and attempt vehicular manslaughter. Or he might have just been sleeping off a buzz.

It was still an easy case, she told herself. Surveillance was always easier than most anything else. But at the moment she was really craving something more challenging.

She turned off the tablet and put it in the passenger seat in anticipation of leaving when she caught movement out of the corner of her eye. Dubov had just walked out of the hotel, hair mussed and chin sporting a thin layer of stubble. If she hadn't seen his tweets she would've assumed that he woke up seconds before appearing on the street.

Dubov crossed directly in front of where she was parked and turned to look through the windshield at her. Ari froze. He continued around to the driver's side and hunched forward so he could still see her as he continued down the sidewalk. Ari kept her eyes locked with his. She couldn't tell if he recognized her, if he had seen her waiting, and she was suddenly very glad the doors were locked.

After holding eye contact far longer than necessary, Dubov's expression flattened into a goofy grin and he said, "Hey!"

Ari nodded, as neutral a response as she could manage.

"You'd look a lot prettier if you smiled."

"Oh, you've gotten be kidding me." She looked away from him and started the engine.

"Don't be stuck-up! I'm just complimenting you."

Ari shook her head. In the side mirror she watched him continue down the street. So the guy was sexist on top of all his other charms. The karaoke bar was going to be an absolute blast.

In another lifetime, Ari had lived in the fancypants Leschi neighborhood in the same house her mother still owned. It was close enough to Lake Washington that Ari could smell the water as she parked at the curb. Coming home still felt strange so she took a moment after parking to gather her thoughts.

She and her mother were friendly now after years of estrangement. She was a grownup now, and she understood things aren't always black and white. She and her mother had fought a war together. They spent holidays together, they emailed, they were even Facebook friends. They'd taken down the man who sired her, the rapist who dedicated his life to hunting *canidae*. Their reunion was eased on its way by Dale, who frequently acted as a buffer between the two stubborn Willow women. It wasn't the perfect mother-daughter relationship, but who really had one of those?

Ari finally got out and went up to the door. Her mother had obviously been watching from a window and answered almost before Ari could lower her hand after knocking. Gwyneth Willow shared her daughter's height and piercing blue eyes. Her thick black hair was bundled into a knot that fell over her shoulder. She was wearing a robe and seemingly nothing else, but Ari wasn't alarmed. Nudity had always been a minor thing when she was growing up. "*Canidae* have to be more comfortable with nudity than other people," Gwyneth explained. "Your pack is going to be full of friends, coworkers, family members. It's natural for us to see each other in all of our natural forms." Ari still believed that, but she also knew it wasn't practical to run around Seattle as a nudist.

"This is a surprise," Gwyneth said. "Is Dale with you?"

"No, she's at home. I wanted to talk with you privately."

"Is everything okay?"

Ari nodded. "I just wanted to get your advice."

Gwyneth raised an eyebrow. "Seriously?"

"Don't make a big deal out of it."

"Of course." She stepped to the side and invited Ari in.

A pair of suitcases were sitting next to the foyer closer. Airport tags dangled from the handles. "Traveling?"

"Uh, yes. Just a quick trip. I got back late last night."

"Anywhere fun?"

Gwyneth avoided eye contact as she brushed past her daughter. "Uh, London."

Ari grimaced and followed her into the living room. "Aha. So. Still seeing Milo?"

"I'm not 'seeing' anybody, Ariadne. But in the interest of full disclosure, yes. I did see Miss Duncan while I was there."

Ari tried to be okay with the revelation as she perched on the arm of her favorite chair. There were so many reasons Milo wasn't right for her mother. She was much too young, for starters. She had been enlisted by Gwyneth and another *canidae* named Ben in a convoluted scheme to break up Ari and Dale. And there was the fact she was a woman. Ari was confused by how big a factor Milo's gender was, but she couldn't help it. Her mother had never hinted at any same-sex attraction, and now she was hooking up with someone young enough to be her daughter? It was unsettling.

Gwyneth sat on the couch, hands flat on her thighs. "I've spent my entire adult life trying to bring down the hunters. I never had time for a social life. Now that wolf manoth has been quashed, I have free time to explore myself. That includes my sexuality. But I doubt you came here to judge me for my choice in casual sex partners, so why don't we just move on?"

"Right." Ari brushed her hands over her thighs. "I got a job offer from GG&M. They want me to be their in-house investigator. I've been on probation with them for the past couple of months and, when that ends, the head partner is going to offer me a full-time job. It would mean giving up Bitches. More importantly it would mean not working with Dale anymore."

"I see. What does Dale think?"

"She doesn't want me to make a decision based on how it affects her. But she's told me how much she loves her job. If I take it away from her..."

Gwyneth said, "You're not necessarily taking it away from her. You're simply moving forward without her."

"Yeah, that sounds much better."

"It would be a promotion? Higher pay?" Ari nodded. "Safer?" Another nod. "Other than Dale's employment, what are the cons?"

Ari said, "I don't like the woman I'd be reporting to. I don't want to report to anyone. I like being my own boss."

"Sure. Who wouldn't. But sometimes you need to think of the future. Dale's feelings might be hurt for a while, but that will blow over. You might be grateful for a larger paycheck in a few years. You could be putting away toward your retirement." She sighed and looked at her feet. "Of course, none of that would be necessary if you would just allow me to take care of you."

"I'm a little old for an allowance."

"Parents help their children, Ariadne. There's no shame in that. And there's no shame in taking a better-paying version of the same job you're doing now. Dale will understand if you make that choice, because she'll understand you're making it for the both of you. If you decide to take the job for more money, it will be so you can better take care of her. She's a smart young woman. And she adores you."

Ari said, "Everything I've built, and that we've built together, would just go away. Bitches would cease to exist."

"Maybe Bitches existed to bring you and Dale together. It gave you an environment to find one another, become friends who grew into lovers. And now that you're a couple, it served its purpose. It can be put to rest."

"Maybe," Ari muttered.

Gwyneth said, "I hope that didn't seem too harsh. I'm extremely proud of everything you've accomplished with your agency. But I feel as though you've already made up your mind to say no. I thought I would play devil's advocate. If it made you angry, well... I'm used to you being angry at me."

"No. You just told me what I haven't been admitting to myself. Maybe I can take the job without ruining what I have with Dale."

Gwyneth laughed and stood up. "Sweetheart, as someone who tried to destroy that relationship - an act for which I am very, very sorry - I can assure you that the bond between you and your partner is as strong as any pack I've ever seen. To break that woman's heart would take an act of cruelty I don't believe you're capable of."

"Thank you, Mom."

Gwyneth kissed Ari's cheek. "Whatever decision you make, now that I'm proud of you."

Ari nodded and stood up. "I should go. I have to follow a hockey player around tonight."

"Be safe."

"Always. And with... your... things... be safe, too."

Gwyneth smiled. "I will."

Ari avoided looking at the suitcases on her way out of the house, hoping ignoring them would speed her erasing their meaning from her brain.

"U guys better not of sent me to one of them queer bars!"

Ari had gone home to have dinner and play nursemaid for Dale while she waited for Dubov to start his night out. She kept an eye on his tweets so she'd know when he was on the way to the karaoke bar. It only took an hour before she felt like she had to wash her phone. The guy couldn't spell, could barely complete a thought, and once he reached Capitol Hill, they became horribly homophobic. "Everything heres RAINBOWS! Even Xwalks r damn RAINBOWS!" and "Pretty soon gona be illegal to be STR8! Just watch!"

Dale elected to stay home due to her injury, but Ari kept her on the phone for the short drive. "Even if he's not the guy who tried to run us over, can't I rough him up a little just on principle?"

"Sure. Get in a few good licks for me."

Ari sneered and looked down the street from where she had

parked. It wasn't much of a crowd yet so she felt confident she could get in even without showing what little cleavage she had available. If Dubov had seen the rainbow crosswalks he had to be close.

"In all honesty," Dale said, "this is exactly the kind of thing the team owners are looking for. Seattle is an extremely gay-friendly city, especially compared to some other franchise cities in the league. If the Totems want someone who will represent the values of the city, they're not going to want this guy who is spewing hatred about queers on his Twitter feed."

"True. So either way, I can put a big red X on his name."

"Exactly."

Dubov rounded the corner, staring down at the phone clutched in hands so big it looked as if he was wearing his uniform gloves. As he approached he stuck the phone into the pocket of his coat.

"He's here. Gotta go."

"Be safe, puppy."

Ari hung up and got out of the car. There was no bouncer or velvet rope blocking the entrance so she walked in, trading the sounds of the street for the overloud music pouring from the speakers and the low hum of chatter. She made her way to the bar and chose a position where she could see both the door and the main stage. Currently a girl dressed unseasonably in a giant scarf and a knit cap was more or less making progress through "Because the Night."

Dubov appeared and was immediately surrounded by the college-aged patrons. He signed autographs and posed for pictures as he slowly inched toward the bar. Ari had been worried he would recognize her from outside the hotel so she'd put on a baseball cap and a pair of thick-framed eyeglasses that she hoped would disguise her enough for a cursory examination. Dubov motioned for the bartender and scanned the crowd. His eyes skipped over her without so much as a hesitation.

Once he got his drink, he made his way to the main stage. "What do you ladies wanna hear, huh? I can do it all. Classic rock? None of that boyband shit. Can't have that showin' up on YouTube, you know? People might talk!"

Ari joined the crowd of adorers. Dubov chose one of the women around him at random and told her to pick what song he would sing. She headed off, beaming with pride at the responsibility she'd been handed, as Dubov took a position near the stage. He remained standing, swaying to the music as the girl finished her song. He applauded and whistled when she finished, then climbed up to take her place.

"All right, everybody, here we go!" The music started he swayed his hips and rocked his head to the beat. Ari recognized the song as "You Make Me Feel Like Dancing," and Dubov's moves fit the disco tune. When he started singing, she was startled when he actually pulled off the falsetto. The women were going nuts, screaming so loud that they almost drowned out his singing. During the first chorus he took off his jacket and tossed it toward an empty seat.

Ari made her way over to where it landed. She moved quickly, dipping down and sliding her hand into the chest pocket. She got the phone out while Dubov was looking the other way. She found a spot against the wall in a dark corner and tapped the screen. There was a passcode, and she held the phone up so she could see smudges on the screen. It was a trick Dale had taught her on the Wilcox case, and she was amazed at how often it worked. It took her four tries but the screen eventually came up and revealed a string of messages between Dubov and someone identified as 'Toto.'

"How late will you be tonight?"

"Hard to say. I'll try not to be long. Why, do you have plans?"

"I can be convinced to cancel any plans that don't involve you."

"Twist my arm. Internet says the karaoke bar you're going to closes at two o'clock. I expect you no later than 2:15."

"I'll be there with bells on."

"Kinky."

She was amazed at how articulate and well-spoken Dubov seemed in his messages. Maybe the character limit really was restricting his natural speech. But she couldn't focus on that now; the song was only about four minutes long, so she didn't have much time to snoop. She went to the photos and saw shots of Puget Sound, the Great Wheel, the Space Needle... all shots that newcomers to the city eventually took. Dubov didn't appear in any of them. She went to the information for "Toto" and quickly memorized the number, went back to messages, and turned the phone off. She dropped it onto the seat as the music ended and Dubov was taking his bows.

She texted Dale the number. "Can you tell me who this belongs to?"

"ASAP," Dale responded. Ari watched someone else take the stage and start singing *Mutt* by Dash Warren. Halfway through the first verse, her phone buzzed with another text from Dale. "Bryan Dunn. He lives in Bothell."

Ari frowned. Her thumb hesitated over the keypad, but there was no point in sending a text requesting confirmation. Dale wouldn't have sent the information if she wasn't sure. The phone might have been registered to Bryan Dunn while being used by his wife or daughter. Maybe an affair or an underage girlfriend?

"What do you know about him?"

"Not a lot. How much do you need?"

She watched Dubov retrieve his jacket. He patted the pocket, visibly tensed, and then grabbed his phone from the spot where she'd dropped it. The look of panic on his face when he checked to see if it was still locked was almost all the confirmation she needed.

"Is there any way you tell if he's gay?"

Another minute passed. Dubov went to get a drink and his adoring public followed.

Dale texted back. "According to Facebook, yes. No H8 pictures, shares lots of liberal posts talking about equality, anti-Trump. Relationship status: it's complicated. So who is he?"

Ari watched as Dubov posed for more pictures.

"I think he's Tyler Dubov's boyfriend."

CHAPTER SEVEN

OVER THE next fifteen minutes, Dale sent Ari a series of pictures of the man she identified as Bryan Dunn. All had been publicly posted to his Facebook and showed him attending various hockey games over the past year. He was always rooting for Dubov's team. Two months earlier, he announced he was moving to Seattle "for work." It was around the same time Dubov was signed to the Totems.

While Ari was looking at the photos, Dubov had grown increasingly antsy and distracted. He was forcing his smiles and refusing offers to get back onstage. Losing his phone, even for a few seconds, seemed to have hardened a shell around him. Ari could see the fear behind his eyes as he clutched the phone in one large hand. It never left his grip and he constantly looked at the screen to make sure it was still locked. She felt bad for causing him such mental anguish. He finally told his hangers-on that he was feeling too tired to keep up and wished them a good night.

She followed him out when he left. A gentle rain had started while they were inside and Ari was grateful for the baseball cap of her disguise. They were almost at the Jimi Hendrix statue, a slender man on his knees and leaning back with the neck of his guitar raised to the heavens, when Dubov cut toward the street. Ari moved between the bumpers of two cars so she could see where he was going.

When she stepped out into the street, he was beside her. His hand went against her throat before she could react, clasping both her hands around his forearm as she was lifted and slammed against the backside of one of the SUVs. He pressed his body against hers so she couldn't squirm free. She tried to kick but he positioned himself so she couldn't get at his groin.

"Who are you?" he said, his face so close to hers she could see the spittle on his bottom lip. "Why are you following me? You were outside my apartment too, right?"

"I'm..." Her voice was a croak. She slapped at his arm. "I can't..."

He released his grip but moved his hand down to her shoulder. He gripped it tight enough to hurt and kept her back against the vehicle.

"My name is Ariadne Willow. I'm a private investigator."

She saw a flash of fear in his eyes. He looked up and down the street as if he expected a mob of reporters to descend. When he confirmed the street was mostly empty, he stepped closer and lowered his voice to a shaky whisper. "Who hired you?"

"Your bosses. The same people who hired you." She didn't want to give away the fact she was investigating the entire team. "People who wouldn't want me to talk too loudly about why you're in Seattle until a certain unveiling."

He was breathing so hard that his shoulders were rising and falling like a bull about to charge. His nostrils flared and plumes of air shot out around his head to make him look like he was in a cartoon.

"Why?"

"They hired me to see what you were hiding. They thought it was something bad."

"And what did you learn, you little bitch? Huh? Snooping in my phone?"

Ari said, "What I found in your phone is nothing compared to what you put up on public forums. All that bigoted shit. Are you overcompensating or are you really that self-hating?"

He moved close again. "You shut your damn mouth or I'll~"

"You'll what?" She swung her arm up and chopped her hand against his elbow. His arm bent and the pressure was removed from her shoulder. She stepped to one side, wrapped her leg around his, and shoved him forward into the space she had just been occupying.

His head bounced off the glass hard enough to make the car alarm chirrup once and then fall silent. Ari put some distance between them, rolling her shoulders in preparation of a fight in case he came after her.

The fight seemed to be washing out of him. He hung his head and she watched the machismo and rage fade. "What are you going to do?"

"Why don't we find somewhere more private to talk about that? Not to mention dryer."

He brushed a hand under his nose, checked it for blood, and nodded. "Okay. Yeah."

Ari said, "Good. There's a diner not far from here."

Even though he looked meek and defeated, Ari made sure to keep an eye on him as she led him away from the karaoke bar.

Lost Lake Lounge was a throwback to another age, a diner-bar-cafe combination that blended elegance and nostalgia in a beautiful balance. The walls were wood paneling with support beams of stone and the floor was a classic black-and-white checkerboard pattern. She'd chosen it because it was nearby and it was open twenty-four hours. She hadn't remembered there were rainbow flags in the window until they arrived, but Dubov didn't seem to notice. He did see the rainbow-colored poster on the door that declared it was a designated Safe Place for victims of LGBT-related crimes.

Once inside Dubov went to the red vinyl booth that was farthest from the door. He dropped heavily as Ari made their drink order from the woman behind the bar: two root beers. When the drinks were ready, she brought them to the table.

"I saw online that this was your favorite drink. Was that a lie, too?"

"No. I like it. Thanks."

"Thanks for pulling your punches back there. I've seen video. You could have put me through that truck without even blinking."

He shrugged and looked at the froth on his drink. "What are you gonna do?"

"There are two options. One, I can go and tell your bosses what I found just on your social media. Bigoted nonsense about queers. That might fly down south, but you're in Seattle now. I know you saw the sign on the door back there. This city stands by all of its citizens, save for bigots like you're pretending to be. Your bosses want players who will represent Seattle well. They take one look at that shit you were posting and you'll be packing your bags for the next port of call. Might be a shame considering you-know-who's life was uprooted to move here for you."

He flinched. "Or?"

"Or you decide to come out on your own. You own up to all the stuff you posted as a cover. More importantly, you apologize for anyone you may have hurt by using that language. A popular athlete like you talking like that? You probably hurt a bunch of people just to keep your secret. That's not right. You probably hid to protect your career, right? Well, you're in Seattle now. The lie is going to do a lot more harm than the truth that you're gay."

"I'm not gay."

Ari rolled her eyes. "Dude..."

"I'm not gay. I'm bisexual. It's a different thing, right?"

"Oh. Yeah, it is."

He sniffled. The rain was dripping out of his hair and trickling over the slope of his forehead. "Couple years ago, I was playing for a San Diego team. I asked them for a hot spot, and some fans thought it would be funny to send me to a gay nightclub. I didn't care. Drinks are drinks, dancing is dancing. What the hell. But I was nervous. I felt out of place. I was afraid everyone would think I was making fun of them, you know? But one guy saw I was having a hard time and came over to make sure no one was teasing me. Weird, right? Big guy like me?"

He chuckled and rubbed his hand under his nose.

"Anyway. He looked out for me the whole night. He made it great. And it was the first time... I mean, you know I'm the enforcer. It's my job to look out for the team. I make sure no one gets hurt. No one takes penalties. No one has to suffer because I take their licks for them. That night with Bry, that was the first time anyone had been looking out for *me*. I didn't want to let that go. At first I was just calling him up to get drinks. Hang out. Then one night we're at my place and I realized I'm not worried about him making a move on me. I'm worried that he might not. So I made a move on him."

Ari smiled. "Sounds like a good guy."

"He told me that my feelings didn't mean I was gay. He explained I was probably bisexual. I always thought that was just the same thing, but now I know better."

"And he puts up with the cover? The pictures with all the women, the hate speech?"

Dubov nodded slowly. "I panicked. I went overboard trying to be the straightest guy possible. I don't even notice half the time until he calls me out on something particularly bad. He hates that Twitter bullshit, but he always tells me he understands. He knows it's for my career. My public persona." He put his hands over his face and rubbed. "I guess that's just another way he's looking out for me, after all this time."

"Maybe it's time you look out for him."

He took a deep breath and looked around the diner. "I've said a lot of bad things. I cried sometimes when I posted it. I had to use a completely different voice just to get the courage to post them. How am I ever going to live that down?"

"It'll take a while," Ari admitted, "but own up to it. Seattle can be a forgiving place if you're sincere with us."

"Are you gay?"

"Yeah, I am."

He nodded slowly. "Bry says he can tell, but I can't. I got no reason to spot the gay guy in a crowd since I have him." He grinned and Ari could suddenly understand why women found him attractive. There might be some broken hearts throughout Seattle when he made his announcement, but they'd get over it.

"I know you probably can't do too much before the official announcement of the team roster," Ari said, "but at least tone down the bigotry and the hate? We get enough of that from the real bigots, we don't need to be doing it to ourselves."

"You got it."

"I'm going to leave you alone now. You probably want to think about what you're going to say to Bryan when you get home."

"Probably should." She started to get out of the booth. "Thanks for the root beer."

"Sure. I'll add it to your boss's bill." He chuckled and bobbed his head. Ari hesitated next to the table. "Can I ask you a question?"

He looked up at her and shrugged.

"Where were you last night?"

Dubov said, "Bryan had a work thing all day yesterday. When he got home he was stressed out, so I made him dinner and we watched a movie."

Ari tried not to look disappointed. "Another question. Your teammates... are there any of them you don't trust? Anyone who might seem a little... shady or unreliable?"

He narrowed his eyes, confused rather than defensive. "I don't know what you mean."

"Are there any you might hesitate to stand up for if they got into trouble?"

"It's my job to protect everyone on the ice, Miss Willow. If they're in a Totems jersey, then I'll lay down in front of the Zamboni for any one of them. No questions asked." He hesitated and sucked his teeth. "But off the ice...? I guess if I saw Lindholm or Aulie getting mugged, I wouldn't cross the street to pull the guy off 'em."

Two members of the Newton Five, Ari noted. She took a card from her wallet and placed it next to his glass. "Thanks, Mr. Dubov. Give me a call if you think of anything else?" He nodded. "And good luck with Bryan. He sounds like a great guy."

"Sure. Maybe it's time I start showing him, huh?"

"That sounds like a great idea." She touched the brim of her hat with two fingers. "You have a good night, Tyler."

"You too."

Ari went home so she could give Dale some tender loving care. All the years of post-transformation massages had more than earned her a full-time nurse, and Ari was prepared to wait on her hand and foot. She stopped at Safeway to get a pint of Dale's favorite ice cream and took it home to her. Dale thanked her with a kiss and allowed Ari to form a nest for her on the couch. Once she was settled in, Ari sat on the floor with the laptop so she could watch game footage of the people she was supposed to be investigating. Her work would be meaningless if they behaved in public but played like assholes.

"Oh, see that file on the desktop?"

Ari minimized the window. "Which?"

Dale reached over her shoulder to point. "That. When you told me about the five guys meeting at the ice rink, I decided to see if they had any connection with each other. I looked back over their careers to see if anyone's time on any team overlapped with anyone else's."

"Damn, sweetie. How long did that take?"

"Time was meaningless today. Just a long boring slog of minutes I had to fill. I hate being sidelined. But it did take a while, so I want proper appreciation from you."

Ari twisted around and stretched to put a kiss on Dale's cheek. "Thank you, Miss Frye."

"You're welcome. I'm not sure if it'll be any help. Aulie and Lindholm were on the Penguins together, but only for about half a season. Oborin was on the Flyers, which was the team where Muldoon made his name all those years ago, so there's a chance they ran into each other there. But none of the others have any crossover."

"I'm still glad to have it." She clicked back to the game videos. She watched the benches to see if any of the Newton Five gravitated toward each other. "Who chose the team? Like was there a person who came in and said 'get me Oesterle and Aulie'?"

"There's a draft," Dale said.

Ari started to get up. "Do you need a blanket?"

Dale chuckled and put a hand on Ari's shoulder. "No, there's a draft where the teams pick the players. They take turns choosing players based on a lottery system."

"So it's like choosing your team on the playground."

"Yes, puppy, it's exactly like that." She stroked the top of Ari's head.

Ari said, "Don't patronize me, woman."

Dale laughed and threaded Ari's hair through her fingers. "Seriously, you know nothing about sports. How do you even call yourself a lesbian?"

"I have other areas of expertise."

"Name one."

Ari put down the laptop with the game tape still running. She lifted the blanket covering Dale's lower body and Dale laughed as her skirt was moved out of the way. She pressed her back against the couch cushion and settled into a more comfortable position as Ari wormed her way between her legs. She sighed, closed her eyes, and smiled as Ari proved her status as an expert where it counted. She rested one hand on top of the lump Ari's head made in the blanket. She turned her head to the side and, when her eyes opened briefly, she saw something on the laptop screen.

"Puppy, stop. Ariadne... stop..."

"What's wrong?"

"Nothing with that." Dale pointed at the computer. "Look. Look, maybe it'll show him again..."

Ari sat up and retrieved the laptop. "Well, it's recorded, babe. We can just rewind it." She licked her lips, face still flush, and tried to focus now that her mind had so dramatically jumped tracks. Dale pointed when she had gone back far enough and Ari hit play.

"Hold on... I'm not sure where exactly he... there! Pause it on him."

Ari froze the image on a shot of the team's bench. Dale pointed at the boulder-shaped man in a charcoal-gray suit standing behind Kristof Oborin. He was watching the game with his arms crossed, face fixed into a scowl. He had a receding hairline, a wide jaw, and features that made Ari think of a grumpy bulldog. Ari was fairly sure she'd never seen him before, but Dale jabbed her finger at him again.

"Who is that?"

"I can look up the coaching staff. Which, uh... which team is the red ones?"

Dale sighed.

"Hey, I just proved my gay credibility."

"Half-proved..."

"You're the one who told me to stop."

"The 'red ones' are the Blackhawks," Dale said, smirking as she rubbed Ari's arm. "This is the 2014 season."

Ari searched for the team's staff and clicked on the official homepage. The man Dale had identified was the second photo in the lineup.

"Vince Halphen, the Blackhawks' assistant coach." She looked at Dale. "You've seen him somewhere before?"

"He was at the restaurant last night. He was sitting at the bar for the last part of our meal, and he got up and left around the time we got the check."

Ari said, "You remember that?"

"He..." She hunched her shoulders and ducked her head shyly. "He looks like a stuffed animal I used to have. I noticed because of that. But he was definitely there, watching us."

"And he left right before we did."

"He saw us getting the check, so he would've known we were about to leave."

Ari said, "He wasn't listed in any of the paperwork I got from GG&M. He might not be involved with the Totems. He could just be... visiting." She couldn't make herself sound convincing. "It is pretty suspicious that he and Oborin are both here at the same time. But maybe that's just our own perception making it seem suspicious."

"I don't think so," Dale said. "I think he's involved. I'm taking it another step and saying that he was watching us and waiting to see when we'd be on the street. I think he was the one driving the truck that tried to run us down."

Ari glared at the man's smiling face. "Well, then I think tomorrow I'm going to find Mr. Halphen and have a little conversation with him."

CHAPTER EIGHT

ARI WAS standing beside the bed in boyshorts and a tank top when her phone rang. Dale was closer to the charger so she pulled the plug and tossed it underhanded to her. Ari caught it and checked the screen before she answered.

"Good morning, Cecily."

"Willow, I want you to speak with you in my office this morning. Sometime before lunch. What time works for you?"

Ari pinned the phone against her shoulder and stepped into her jeans. "Can't do it. I have an appointment that might take all morning."

"Cancel it."

Ari smirked. "Sorry. Hopefully whatever your thing is will wait."

"My thing won't wait, Miss Willow. When we made this arrangement, you agreed that any cases I brought you would take precedence over what you were working on at the time. If you choose to break that agreement, then--"

"Hold on," Ari said. "I'm doing that. The case I'm working on was brought to me by someone at your firm. I dropped everything and I've been focusing entirely on that, just like we said I would."

Cecily was silent for a moment. "Who brought you the case?"

"Eric Wiseman."

"Hold."

Ari rolled her eyes as music began playing. "Unbelievable." She watched as Dale maneuvered herself off the mattress with the crutch. "Do you need help?"

"No, I want to get the hang of this. I'll get good at it by the time I'm healed."

The music cut off as Dale limped into the bathroom. Cecily said, "It would seem you are correct, Miss Willow. I apologize for the miscommunication. Continue on your current investigation."

"Sure." Ari hung up and dropped the phone on the bed. "Are you okay in there?"

Dale called back, "Making it work!"

They'd agreed that with Dale's injury, it would be too hard for them to share the shower. It would be difficult enough for Dale to position herself so the bandaged ankle was out of the stall without worrying about a whole other person. Ari went to the bathroom door and bumped it open as she buttoned her shirt.

"Are you going to work from home again?"

Dale poked her head around the curtain, her hair a wet, spiked mess. "I was thinking about driving in to the office, just to see how irritating this damn crutch makes things. Why?"

"If you were going to stay, I could take the car. But I can wait until you're finished and drop you off. I have plenty of time."

"You sure?"

Ari nodded. "Just promise me that if the office is too much of a hassle, you'll either call me for a ride or Uber home."

"I promise."

Dale disappeared back behind the curtain and Ari went out into the living room. A thought occurred to her and she went up the stairs to the door between their apartment and the main house where Neka Teller lived. She knocked, unsure if Neka had headed off to classes or work, but Neka answered quickly. She was dressed in sweats and had earbuds hanging off the collar. It was strange to think of her as a landlord, since she was so much younger than them. She was a student at the University of Washington and currently in the process of building her own boat from the ground up.

"Hey, Ariadne. What's up?"

"Hey. Sorry to bother you. I was just wondering if we could inconvenience you for a while. Dale hurt her ankle, so showering is going to be tough until~"

Neka interrupted her. "My bathtub! You want to borrow my

bathtub? Of course. I broke my leg a couple years ago. Showering was all but impossible. I can't imagine trying to shower in that stall downstairs. You guys have a spare key, so whenever you need it. I mean, if we're home~"

It was Ari's turn to interrupt. "We'll obviously knock first. But thanks, Neka, I really appreciate it. I know Dale will, too."

"Absolutely."

"I'll let you get to your run."

Neka nodded. "You guys have a good day."

Ari went back downstairs. Dale was out of the shower and partially dressed. Ari explained to her about the arrangement to use Neka's bathroom and Dale sighed. She rolled her head back, eyes closed, and sighed with relief.

"That's amazing. Thank you, puppy."

"Sure." She bent down and kissed Dale's hair. "Frozen waffles or picking something up on the way in?"

"Picking up something else. I want some coffee."

"Works for me. I'll get everything together." On her way out of the bedroom, Ari called over her shoulder, "You look really good in my shirt."

"This is my shirt."

"You bought it for me, though. Right?"

"It looks better on me."

Ari grinned. "Can't argue that."

She hadn't lied on the phone with Cecily; she planned to drive out to Tukwila where Vince Halphen lived and where the Totems would have their arena. Rink. Arena?

"Baby," she called, "is hockey in a rink or an arena?"

"Arena."

They picked up breakfast on the way to the office, with Ari waiting in line and bringing Dale her order, and then Ari headed out for Tukwila. She tried to put all the pieces together as she drove south. She hadn't seen Halphen at the restaurant, but she trusted Dale's word as much as her own. If he was in Seattle, he had to be taking a high-level job with the Totems. He would be the assistant coach under Muldoon, most likely. So Muldoon and Halphen, with Aulie, Oesterle, Lindholm, and Oborin were involved with something big. Big enough to attempt vehicular homicide, and yet not so big that it would show up even after she and Dale started looking for it.

Tukwila was a relatively small suburb of Seattle, but every road and railroad seemed to congregate there before pouring into the big city. Boeing Field was the crown on the city's head and SeaTac was nestled between them and Puget Sound. The convenience was most likely the reason they'd been chosen as the Totem's new home.

Ari found the apartments where Halphen lived, a pretty enough group of dun-colored condos that looked disturbingly similar to some cult compounds she'd seen on the news. As nice as it might have been, it was still a far cry from Muldoon's estate in Medina. Her plan was to get into Halphen's apartment so she could get a whiff of his scent. Hopefully she could compare it to the miasma she'd gotten when she found the abandoned truck. But if Halphen was the driver, she had to be very careful not to be seen. She parked where her car couldn't be seen from the condos and walked back, tucking her hair under a baseball cap before pulling her hoodie up over it. The weather was just cold enough to justify the outfit so she wouldn't seem overly suspicious as she approached the property.

Ari used the trees for cover as she approached. Halphen's registered vehicle, when he wasn't stealing trucks to run down pesky detectives, was a beige 2010 Honda Insight. She didn't see a vehicle matching that description so she had to assume he wasn't home. A quick pass revealed his entire unit seemed to be abandoned for the workday, so she risked a quick stroll through the interior to figure out which unit belonged to her quarry. His mailing address listed his unit as Number 5, so all she had to do was figure out the numbering system. Once it was located she went back outside and climbed over the waist-high railing onto his deck. Halphen had a barbeque grill which reeked of charcoal and ruined meat standing guard over a rusted bicycle and patio furniture that looked like it had been passed down through at least four generations.

She ignored the debris and focused on the lock. She didn't want to literally break anything if she didn't have to, and the lock cooperated by being ridiculously easy to jimmy. She pushed the sliding door shut behind her to block out any nature smells that might have interfered with her smell-identification. She moved toward the couch and focused on the cushion that had obviously seen the most use. She sniffed as she went past, picking up a definite trace of the man who lived there. It was good, but she knew where the strongest odors would be lurking.

At the end of the hall, she found what was definitely the bedroom of a bachelor. Unmade bed under a window shaded by ratty curtains, clothes overflowing from the hamper in the corner, and a collection of porn on DVD next to the boxy television. It was nice to know some people were still relatively old-school when it came to getting off.

Ari closed the door and settled in the center of the room. It would be better if she was the wolf, but transforming would make escape nearly impossible if someone happened to come home. Her senses were heightened even when she was in human form, so she closed her eyes and focused on what she had smelled the other night in the parking garage. There had been dozens of scents and while, at the time, the wolf probably could have sorted them all out into individuals, she was working with faded memory and what was basically hearsay from a completely different side of her brain.

"There was," she whispered, "cloves and cinnamon and perfume, cologne, body odor, pine needles, no that's not important, there was... cigarettes, smashed under leather, and dirt and oil stains, oil from the cars, no, forget that." She was barely aware she was speaking aloud. She breathed in and let the air out through her mouth. There was something, something small, something...

She opened her eyes and looked around the room. A glass jar of cologne called Creed Aventus. She'd never heard of it, but she sprayed a bit in the air and her mind instantly twigged back to the parking garage. "Oak moss," she whispered, "vanilla, pineapple, apples." She took out her phone and looked up the name. It was an extremely expensive cologne, she discovered, so the odds of a coincidence were incredibly small. Small enough that she was willing to discount the possibility entirely. She looked at the jar accusingly as if she could see Halphen in it.

"You were there. You were the driver, you son of a bitch."

She was standing in the home of the man responsible for hurting Dale, and the urge to make him pay was almost overwhelming. She knew that doing so would only announce that she'd been there, and she didn't want to tip her hand yet. She looked at the cologne, the three-hundred-dollar bottle of stinky water, and went into the bathroom. She poured half of what was left into the sink under running water to hopefully mask the scent, then refilled it with tap water. It was petty, yes, but it made her feel good as she returned it to the bedroom.

She spent close to an hour searching the apartment for anything that might clue her in to what Muldoon and the other four were up to. She still hadn't definitively connected the hit-and-run with the group she'd seen at the Newton Rink, but the two were just unusual enough that she felt they had to be related. Halphen knew Oborin and now they were both employed by the Totems, and Oborin was having a secret meeting with the coach at an ice rink frequented by kids and suburban moms. She'd been hired to find something fishy in the team, and she had a feeling she'd found it.

Whatever was going on behind the scenes, there wasn't anything in Halphen's condo to enlighten her. She left through the front door just in case anyone was watching and trekked through the woods back to the car. Once she was safely behind the wheel, she took out her phone and called Dale.

"Bitches Investigations."

"He's the guy. Good job, Miss Frye."

Dale said, "Awesome. I'll give myself a gold star for the day!"

"Give yourself two."

"Since I have you on the phone, I found something, too. Max Janus, one of the team's goalies. Five years ago, a little girl with cancer asked Make-a-Wish for an autograph from him. He came through with a signed helmet, pads, a poster, and a pair of skates. He showed up at the hospital and watched a game with her. When the day was over, he pulled the parents aside and gave them a check to help with her treatment and their expenses. Media didn't find out about it until a few weeks later when the parents wrote a Facebook post."

Ari said, "Wow. That's impressive."

"Yeah. I just thought that after digging for the worst in all these players, you might be craving something that'll make your soul feel good. Whatever Muldoon and his four cronies are involved with, there are some amazing people on the team."

Ari closed her eyes. "Thank you for thinking of that, sweetie. It never even occurred to me, but it was exactly what I needed to hear."

"Any time. So now that you know who came after us, what's your plan?"

Ari thought for a moment before she answered. "Track Halphen, if I can find him. If I can't, I'll switch focus to one of the other Newton Five."

"Be careful. They know what you look like and already tried to take you out once."

Ari shuddered, suddenly grateful Cecily had loaded the office with extra security measures. "Watch your back, too. Hard to run with a bum ankle."

"I'll be careful if you are."

"Deal."

Ari put the phone down and drove back the way she'd come. At the moment she didn't care about the Totems. She didn't even particularly care about what Muldoon was up to or making herself look good for Cecily and GG&M. Her sole purpose for the time being was finding Halphen and making him pay for what he'd done to them. Once she'd done that, solving the rest of it would just be icing on the cake.

CHAPTER NINE

ONCE DALE was entrenched in the office, it was easier to stay in her chair and use the crutch as an oar to get around. Before she left for Tukwila, Ari had taken the whiteboard off the wall and propped it up so Dale could access it without standing up. She had pictures of every potential Totems player taped along the long side with a row of information they'd managed to uncover about them. Muldoon and the rest of what Ari was calling the "Newton Five" were grouped on the left-hand side. All of their info was written in red marker, while everyone else got a neutral blue.

She pushed her chair close and wrote under Halphen's name: "A-hole SOB driver who hurt my foot!" She underlined it twice and glared at the picture she'd downloaded from the website. "Asshole," she muttered. She put the rubber tip of the crutch against the wall and shoved off, using her good foot to steer the chair back around the desk.

Ari texted her when she got back into city limits to say she would spend the rest of the day sniffing around to see if she could find out what Halphen had been up to since arriving in Seattle. Dale didn't envy her the legwork; it would involve talking to a lot of people who wouldn't remember anything clearly, and that was only if she found anyone willing to talk.

Of course, Ari thought that Dale's side of the investigations was mind-numbingly dull. It was anything but boring to Dale. Finding a hint of a trail somewhere online and following it through public records, then tying things together with a piece from this website and a bit from that website was like working a word puzzle that had been spread across the entire internet. It was fun and she found it exciting to build an actual narrative from the fragments she found.

Ari came back to the office for lunch. They talked about their respective progress in digging up facts - Dale had fleshed out a few more of the players, while Ari was still stumped about how Halphen had been filling his time since coming to Seattle - and Ari massaged Dale's ankle.

"Have you called the police yet to tell them about Halphen being the driver?"

Ari shook her head. "I wanted to go to them with something more believable than matching his smell. Even if I told them that, I'd have to admit I'd broken into his place. If I don't find anything solid by tonight, I'll go to Diana. She'll help me figure out what to report."

"Is she okay?" Dale asked.

"As far as I know. Why?"

"She's sounded strange the past couple of times we talked."

Ari said, "Tired? Strung out?" Dale nodded. "I noticed that, too. I'll bring it up tonight if it's not awkward." She looked at her phone to see what time it was. "I should head out. Another few wonderful hours of talking to bartenders who won't remember serving Halphen and knocking on doors of people who are still at work."

"Poor puppy."

They kissed goodbye and Dale went back to her work. Her next target was Yann Olsson, a big Scandinavian ruffian who looked like a cross between Thor from the Marvel movies and Seth Rogen. Olsson came to the Totems from the Senators, for whom he had played since graduating high school. He was twenty-three but built like a house, a monster with the bright smile of a five-year-old. He lived with his parents in Ottawa until he made the move to Seattle. No college, no criminal record, not even a DUI to his name. She went on Tumblr and found a devoted following dedicated to "Yummy Yann." The first picture she found showed him crouching on a downtown street with his arm around a little girl wearing his Senators jersey.

"Yann Olsson," she said, "welcome to the 'good guy' pile. Seattle will be lucky to have you."

She made a note and looked at the whiteboard, scanning the names she had yet to dig deep on. Green, Hamilton, Campbell, Vlcek, Gladstone, Neely. There was a chance one of them would end up being a horrible monster but she had a feeling Ari had found the dark side of the team at Newton Ice Rink. Still, it was their job to clear everybody, so she picked one name at random and started over again.

It was after dark when Ari parked in front of Diana Macallan's home. Their relationship with the detective was complicated. She and Ari had dated until Ari did something stupid to betray her trust. For a few years after their breakup, Diana kept running into Ari while she was half-naked in public looking like a strung-out junkie. She was positive Ari was an addict who refused to get help. Ari had finally revealed her true nature during the wolf manoth case and, in the year and a half since, Diana had become one of their strongest allies on the force.

Ari went up onto the porch and lifted her hand, but stopped herself before she knocked. The curtain on the window looking into the living room was open and she could see Diana's wife, Lucy, slumped asleep on the couch with a book lying open on her chest. Knocking would wake her up and Ari didn't want to disturb the household any more than necessary. She hesitated and then left the porch to walk around the side of the house.

The kitchen window was also open. Diana was standing at the kitchen counter with her back to the window. Ari tapped on the glass to get her attention. Diana turned and her shoulders jumped at the sight of Ari's pale face looming out of the darkness. Ari put a finger to her lips and motioned with her head toward the front of the house. Diana rolled her eyes and started through the house. Ari walked back to the porch.

Through the window she saw Diana enter the living room. She looked toward the couch and saw Lucy asleep, and some of the irritation seeped out of her features as she walked to the door, turned on the porchlight, and slipped outside.

"That was kind. Thank you."

"Of course." The porch was too narrow for them to get very far from the window, so Ari gestured toward the street. "Let's take a walk."

Diana nodded. Ari looked surreptitiously at Diana, worried that she looked even more strung out than she'd sounded on the phone.

She was wearing an old T-shirt, the collar stretched out around her neck, and she had more gray hairs sprouting from the center part than she had last time Ari had seen her. She also looked very, very tired. She kept her gaze forward as they reached the sidewalk and turned right toward the cross-street.

"So what's going on?" Ari asked.

"A lot of stuff."

"Okay. You don't have to be more specific if you don't want to, but..."

Diana pressed her lips together and swallowed. "Lucy hasn't been feeling well lately. The past few weeks, in fact. I finally convinced her to see a doctor. Cancer."

Ari grunted and reached out to touch Diana's arm. "Is... what's... h-how bad is it?"

"It's one of the treatable ones, so at least there's that."

"How's she doing?"

"She doesn't want to draw anymore. The thing she loved more than anything, and she can't do it anymore. And that frustrates her, so she takes it out on me. And I know why she's doing it but it still pisses me off so I take it out on her and I feel like shit and..." She took a deep, shuddering breath and put a hand over her face. Ari moved closer and hugged her. "We've been fighting a lot. She's going through the worst time in her life and I'm supposed to be her safe place."

Ari said, "I know. When my transformations were hurting me so badly it looked like I'd be paralyzed in a few years, Dale and I had our fair share of fights. She would try to help me and I would accuse her of smothering me. She'd leave me alone and I would be mad that she didn't care I was hurting. Stuff like this makes you feel weak and vulnerable and all you want to do is save yourself. So someone offering to help... sometimes it makes you lash out. I know that's what I was doing, even though I didn't realize it at the time. What I did realize, and what I remember about that time now, is how strong Dale was. I know it must have been hell for her, too, but she never let it take her down."

Diana sniffled. "Dale's a tough nut."

"So are you. So is Lucy. Give Dale a call, talk to her about this. I don't know if she'll be able to help, but she's been through it before. And sometimes it helps just to talk."

"Yeah. Just telling you has felt like a weight off." She wiped at her cheeks. "So... go ahead. Whatever you came here for, out with it. Background check? License plate?"

Ari said, "Oh. Actually I came here to give you some information."

"Wow, that's a change of pace."

"Yeah. The truck that tried running me and Dale over the other night. The driver was named Vince Halphen. He has a condo in Tukwila." She handed over the information she'd written down. She'd been cupping the card in her hand, all but forgotten after Diana's news. "I'd like to be there when you talk to him. If that's okay."

Diana angled the card so it caught the glow of a nearby streetlight. "I'll bring him in tomorrow. Thank you. Not just for this..."

"Any time. Anything you need. If Diana ever needs a ride to or from treatment, we're just a call away."

Diana nodded her gratitude and gestured toward the house. "We should head back before she wakes up." They turned and started back. "So how much of the evidence against this guy did you get while you were on all fours? Oh, god. That sounded filthy."

Ari laughed. "Actually none. There's a slight matter of breaking and entering."

"Of course."

"And a good amount of my evidence against him would be hard to explain under oath. I do have an extremely acute sense of smell, but..."

Diana said, "Gotcha. The important thing is that we know who to look for. I'll go over security footage tomorrow and see if I spot him. I'll let you know if we get lucky."

"Thanks."

They were halfway back to the house when Diana's phone rang. She smiled before she answered. "Hello, Lou."

The street was quiet enough that Ari could hear Lucy's response. "I woke up and you were gone."

"I know. I'm sorry. Ariadne came by and we went for a walk so we wouldn't disturb you. We're on our way back now."

"Hurry."

Diana's expression turned serious. "Are you okay?"

"I'm fine. I just..." She trailed off.

"We're almost there." Diana's voice was tender. "I can see the porch from here."

"Okay. Love you."

"Love you, too."

When she hung up, Ari said, "I think you two are going to be just fine."

Diana reached out and bumped Ari's hand with hers. "When you and I broke up, it was because you were immature and self-centered. You used me for information on a case. But you've really grown up the past few years. I don't even recognize the woman I went out with when I look at you."

Ari said, "Dale's influence. I think you and I both ended up exactly where we're supposed to be."

"I hope so."

Lucy came out onto the porch as the approached the house. She lifted her hand in greeting to Ari, who returned the gesture.

"Evening, Lucy. Sorry for borrowing your lady."

"Just as long as you bring her back in one piece."

Diana turned to Ari. "I'll give you a call when we track this guy down."

"I'd appreciate it."

Ari waved to Lucy again and watched Diana head up the walk. She slipped an arm around Lucy's waist and led her back into the house.

Ari picked Dale up at the office and drove her home. At the streetlight on Madison, Ari glanced over to see Dale seemed pensive.

"Everything okay?"

"Fine. I just..." She shrugged. "Usually when we're both in the car, I drive. We never agreed on that or made it a rule. It's just something that happens. And now because of my stupid ankle... I didn't think I'd miss it, but I do."

Ari reached over and rubbed Dale's leg before the light turned green. "Lucy has cancer."

Dale's head snapped back to look at her. "No."

"It's why Diana's been so weird lately. It's really taking its toll on them."

"Oh my God." She was silent for the next block. "Does she need anything? Rides to treatment?"

Ari said, "I already offered. They know we're available if they need us."

Dale nodded. "Good." She looked out the window at the passing buildings. "Everything that happened after your transformations, with the pain you were in... if Diana ever needs someone to listen or just to vent at..."

"I offered that, too." She took Dale's hand. "Did I ever thank you for everything you did back then?"

Dale brought Ari's hand to her lips and kissed the back of it. "Frequently and in myriad ways. But it never hurts to hear your appreciation."

Ari smiled.

When they got home, Ari let Dale lean on her until she got the crutch situated under her arm. "I swear I'm going to get rid of this thing as soon as possible. If I have to learn how to walk on my hands..."

They walked together around the house. Ari stayed within arms' reach just in case Dale needed her help. "If push comes to shove, we'll find you a little cart and the wolf will pull you wherever you need to go."

"That actually sounds awesome. Let's do that tomorrow."

The back porch light was on and, as they reached the top of the stairs, Neka stepped outside. "Hey, I thought I saw you two pull up. The bathroom is going to be free for a while if you wanted to come up and take a bath."

Dale said, "Thank you. I think I'll take you up on that. I just need to get some things."

"No rush. Hey, Ari."

"Hey, Neka."

Ari helped Dale into the apartment, where she proceeded to get the thing she would need for her bath. Ari sat on the edge of the bed and watched.

"When did you know you were going to stay with me?"

Dale looked at her through the bathroom door. "What?"

"Earlier. When we were fighting. You said that there were times when you considered leaving. Me, the agency, everything."

"Well, I'd happened across a sexy, gay, werewolf, private investigator. I'd have been stupid to walk away from that sort of life."

Ari chuckled but tilted her head to the side. "Come on. Seriously."

Dale sighed and thought for a moment. "When I saw that you were helping people. You weren't just spying on people having affairs in cheap hotels. You were taking clients who had nowhere else to turn. Do you remember the woman whose husband stopped sending in child support and disappeared? You tracked him down in the Cascades, camping out in the middle of nowhere. No one but a wolf could have followed his trail. And no one but you would've gone to all that trouble in exchange for a week of home-cooked meals. But I knew even you couldn't do it alone. I knew if I stayed with you, we could really help a lot of people. And we have."

Ari stood up and put her arms around Dale's waist. They kissed for a long moment, Dale leaning on her instead of the crutch. When they pulled back, Ari brushed the hair away from Dale's face.

"I'm not going to take Cecily's offer. Bitches is more than just a job, and I can't throw it all away for a steady paycheck, even if it means you would be safer. There will always be people who need us, and they'll never find us if I'm stuck behind a desk at GG&M. I'm right where I need to be."

"Good." Dale pecked the corners of Ari's mouth. "Me too."

They held each other for another moment before Ari let her go upstairs. She was alone in the apartment and she opened the computer to look at their Totems file. The Newton Five, plus Halphen. There might be some other bad eggs on the team, but she had a feeling those six men deserved the brunt of her attention. Something big was lurking there. It was only a matter of time before she figured out what it was.

CHAPTER TEN

VINCE HALPHEN was seated in the outdoor dining area, a table most likely chosen to avoid the university students gathered inside. He was wearing a baseball cap pulled low over his eyes, hunched over his plate. Ari had gotten a glimpse of the menu and knew the place was more high-brow than she'd have expected from Halphen, but she was still surprised when she saw what he was eating when she sat across from him.

"Roasted bone marrow, Halphen? Damn. I figured your idea of fine cuisine was getting the Quarter Pounder Deluxe at McDonald's."

He glared at her. She'd kept her sunglasses on so he could only see his own face reflected back at him. She could see that he was struggling with how to respond. She could already tell he knew who she was. All that remained to discover was if he'd admit to it.

"Trying to have a meal here, lady."

It would seem not. "Halphen, I'm hurt. You really don't recognize me? I was trying to have a meal myself a few nights ago. You were there, watching me and my girlfriend. Then you tried to run us over with the truck you stole."

Halphen pushed away from the table and stood up. "You're delusional."

Diana was blocking his escape. She lifted her badge and

gestured for him to sit down again. "If you're finished with your meal, maybe we could have a discussion. I'm Detective Macallan. I believe you already know Miss Willow."

He hesitated for a long moment before he resigned himself to sitting back down.

Diana sat next to Ari on the other side of the table. "I saw you in a movie recently, Mr. Halphen. Kind of low-quality, but still not bad. It shows you half a block from a truck that got stolen a few nights ago. You walk toward the truck and, a few minutes later, it comes rolling down the street and you're nowhere to be seen. That's a bit peculiar. Then there's the fact that later the same night, Miss Willow's girlfriend spotted you watching them at the restaurant just before they were almost run over by that stolen truck."

"Sounds pretty, uh, circumstantial to me."

Diana shrugged. "There's also the fact that you're involved with a case Ariadne happens to be working. Those three facts together - your proximity to the truck, your presence at the restaurant, and your connection to her investigation - are enough to bring you in."

Halphen said, "No, it's not."

"Well, maybe not. But my captain trusts me enough to give me a little leeway." She crossed her arms on the edge of the table and leaned forward. "So? Come on. We know you were driving the truck. It's only a matter of time before we have your fingerprints. Whoever drove the truck wiped it down, but there are still loads of prints all over it. You absolutely sure you got them all, Mr. Halphen? Because if not, and we put you in that truck, you're in for a heap of hurt."

He worked his lips, furrowed his brow, and twisted his neck to look toward the street. Ari watched his fingers as he rubbed them against the pad of his thumb. Her mind kept replaying the night outside the restaurant. The pain in her shoulder when she hit the pavement because Dale tackled her out of the way. How goddamned close they had come to one or both of them dying. She dug her thumbnail into her thigh to keep from jumping across the table and throttling him.

"All right. I was in the truck. I tried to run 'em down."

Diana was thrown by the confession, but she covered her surprise well enough that Ari was sure Halphen didn't notice. "Now we're getting somewhere. Why did you do it?"

"I saw the two ladies eating together. Made me sick. Ain't right, two ladies like that, oughta be with men. That's the way it's always been."

Diana sliced her hand through the air over the table. "No, stop right there. Don't make this a hate crime thing. Hate crimes happen every day in this city, and I won't have you belittle those victims by using it as an alibi. This wasn't a crime of passion. This wasn't some random run-in. You stole that truck and then you waited until the perfect moment to run these women down. If they hadn't been on a tree-lined street, you may have succeeded. I want an honest answer from you, Halphen."

He glared at her.

"You just confessed to attempted murder. What have you got to lose?"

"I'm not saying another word without my lawyer present."

Diana sighed and took out her handcuffs. "That means an all-expense paid trip downtown. Pay for your meal before I read your rights."

"And leave a decent tip," Ari added. "This place might be high-dollar, but that doesn't mean their staff sees any of it in their paycheck."

Ari left the restaurant and waited by Diana's car. She watched the other patrons sneak pictures as the cuffs were put on and Halphen was led through the maze of tables and chairs. The urge to attack was still strong. She could feel the wolf side of her personality clawing at her brain insisting she let it take over. The wolf would know how to repay the man for what he'd done. For the briefest moments, she was tempted to let it out. The only thing that kept her from surrendering was the knowledge of how much trouble it would cause Diana.

Diana put him in the backseat and stood next to Ari. "You okay?"

"Yeah. I'll go to the gym, punch a bag or something."

"You might want to call Dale before you do that. If there are five other people involved in whatever this is, they might escalate now that their buddy has been caught. They might come after you both again. Be extremely careful, Ariadne."

"Yes, ma'am." She looked past Diana at Halphen, who was stewing in the backseat. "What's going to happen to him?"

"He confessed to a pretty big charge. He's definitely going to do time."

"Yeah. But he lied about why he did it. That's pretty suspicious."

"You bet it's suspicious. I'll keep pushing him, but with the lawyer in play, I doubt we'll get anything useful. Sorry."

Ari shrugged. "You did your job. That's all anyone can ask of you." She looked past Diana at Halphen. "Whatever Muldoon is up to, it's big enough to justify Halphen sacrificing himself to protect everyone else."

"What would make you fall on your sword for an attempted murder charge?"

Ari shook her head. "I don't know. Protecting someone else, probably. Maybe he assumed he would be going down no matter what happened, so he just sacrificed himself. If that's true, he's not going to roll over on anyone else who was involved."

Diana said, "What's your actual case?"

"Look into the hockey team, see if anyone has any skeletons in their closet. I was brought in to look for DUIs or racist Facebook posts. Dale's still looking into that, but I'm going to focus on this group. I think whatever they're up to is more important."

"Right. Let me know if you find anything or if you need any help."

Ari hesitated.

"I'm a detective no matter what's going on in my personal life. Lucy will understand if I have to back you up."

"Okay. I'll keep your number handy."

"You'd better. I'm taking this guy in. What are you going to do?"

"First I'm going to take care of Dale. Then I'm going to GG&M. The guy who put me on the case needs to know the depth of the shit he's dumped me into."

"And where exactly would I go?" Dale asked when Ari arrived at the office.

"My mother's place," Ari said. "We'll swing by the apartment and pack a bag."

Dale didn't even look away from her computer. "No. I'm not running and hiding."

Ari's shoulders sagged. "These assholes have proven how far they're willing to go."

"Right." Dale finally looked up at her. "So either they'll come here or they'll find out where we live and attack there. Remember when the hunters burned down your apartment? Your neighbors were lucky they weren't hurt. What about Neka? If these hockey players come after you again, they'll find her there and she won't know what hit her."

Ari said, "So take her with you to Mom's…"

"No. You're not the only one who can protect people, Ariadne. I'll let you take me home, but I'm going to stay there to keep an eye on Neka. I'll make sure no one burns down our home."

Ari walked around the desk and bent down to kiss the top of Dale's head. "I'm supposed to be the protector."

"Big bad wolf." Dale reached up and slipped her hand under Ari's shirt. She rubbed the warm skin of Ari's hip. "You take care of what you have to take care of. Neka and I will be fine."

"I'll try to be safe if you do the same."

Dale grinned. "Deal. Now if you really want to feel useful, help me get out to the car so I don't have to use my crutch."

Ari left the elevator and crossed the waiting room without breaking stride. Shannon looked up and tracked her to the doors. "Miss Parrish really is in court at the moment. If you're planning to wait, you'll be here for a very long time."

"I'm not seeing her this time."

Eric Wiseman looked up as she entered his office. "Cecily was right. You really do just barge in whenever you like."

She sat down across from him. "Your boys are going to be short two coaches when they announce their roster."

"What are you talking about?"

"Vince Halphen just got arrested for attempted murder."

Wiseman blanched. "Are you joking?"

"No. My girlfriend and I were the intended victims. Halphen came after me when he caught wind I was investigating the team. But I don't think it was his idea. He rolled over way too easy when the cops came for him, so that makes me think he was just following orders. Take out the nosy private eye, then fall on his sword if anyone connects the dots. Who do you think would have enough power over Halphen to make him do that?"

"Conor Muldoon." He was staring at the desk, eyes wide and unblinking.

"Either him or the owners, but since they're the ones who hired me…"

Wiseman shook his head. "This is far more than I expected you to find, Miss Willow. You must understand I never intended for you or your loved ones to be in any danger, let alone–"

"Save it, Wiseman," Ari said. "What's done is done. I just want to know who else is involved."

"How would I know that? I had no idea Mr. Halphen was a criminal."

"But you knew he was joining the team?" Wiseman nodded slowly. "Who hired him? Muldoon?"

Wiseman nodded again. "As far as I know. I wasn't really privy to that part of the process."

Ari said, "Who are the owners?"

"There's one major shareholder. Ike Levitt."

Ari couldn't hide her surprise. "Seriously? Wow, that guy owns…"

"A little bit of everything," Wiseman said. "Shares in the Seahawks, Mariners, the Sounders, the Storm, and even a couple of teams in Portland and Chicago. He bought the Totems because he wanted to be the high man on the… well… He wanted to be the guy in charge for once."

"Would he have brought in any players?"

Wiseman shook his head. "I highly doubt it. He's a businessman. He can look at stats, but he would entrust the draft to the coach he hired."

Ari said, "And Muldoon is a good coach?"

"He's got a fantastic record, yes."

"So maybe Levitt hired Muldoon on the up-and-up, just brought him in to coach a hockey team, and whatever side things might be going on… that's just Muldoon. He recruited the people he needed for… whatever he's doing."

Wiseman shrugged and held his hands out. "And what might that be?"

Ari stood up. "I don't know. Something big enough that Halphen was willing to fall on his sword to protect it."

"Just… reassure me that the rest of the team is clean."

"So far so good. A lot of Boy Scouts. The rest of the team might have a few DUIs. If anything is going to bring down the team, it's going to be whatever Muldoon's got going."

Wiseman looked deflated, his eyes glassier and less focused than when she'd entered the office. "Right. Of course. Please keep me informed."

She nodded and left the office.

Shannon looked up when she came out. "What, no coffee?"

"Next time I'll bring you a scone to make up for it."

"Gluten-free. They have a special plate for them."

"I promise."

The elevator doors closed on her. She took out her phone and checked social media for updates from her prime suspects. Nothing from Aulie since the night before. Lindholm hadn't posted anything new in weeks. But Oesterle had checked in at a rink in Tukwila ten minutes earlier to "get in some ice-time." Ari checked her watch and decided traffic would probably be cooperative enough for her to arrive before he left.

"Anton Oesterle," she muttered, "get ready for your close-up."

Chapter Eleven

The rink where Oesterle checked in turned out to be the "official home of the Seattle Totems!" according to the banner strung across the front entrance. It was on a hill overlooking Green River, not far from Halphen's condo. Ari doubted they would let her wander in and watch a practice so she parked in front of a nearby department store and walked through the woods to come up at the rink's back side. It was almost completed, but she spotted a pair of trucks from a construction company parked alongside an HVAC van.

No one seemed to be around so she peeked into the back of one truck and snagged a tool belt, a hard hat, and a pair of safety glasses. She put everything on and went inside, glad she had chosen an outfit from the "butch" side of her closet that morning. She hoped the HVAC guys thought she was with the construction company and vice versa. She tugged the belt higher on her waist and slipped in through a maintenance door which had been propped open with a cinder block.

She was in a dark corridor that curved off to either side; she randomly went left knowing it would circle back around eventually. She found a flight of stairs that were only partially completed, ducked under the caution tape, and carefully ascended on the unfinished risers. As expected, the stairs led into a private box that was awaiting chairs, a glass front, and drywall. The shape of the room was framed out by skeletal studs that made the eventual high-dollar boxes look like a row of cages. She moved across the bare floor as quietly as possible, pulling off the hard hat and carefully putting down the belt so the tools wouldn't make noise as she moved.

Ari crouched next to the half-wall overlooking the rink. The Totems were on the ice, half in green jerseys and half in white. None of the jerseys had names, so she couldn't tell if any of the Newton Five were currently active. Muldoon was there, watching from the bottom row of bleachers. He had a notebook open on his lap, pen clutched in his right hand as he rested his chin on the left. Every now and then he would shout something to the players. "You're off-sides, Campbell! Watch that. Is anyone gonna play some defense today? Nice save, Neely!"

Ari stayed low enough that only the very top of her head would be visible from the ice, and even that was mostly hidden by shadows. Still, she had only been in position for a few minutes when the goalie turned to look toward the box. She couldn't make out his face through the grill of his mask, but he seemed to be scanning the row of empty windows for something. Or someone. Ari remained completely still so as not to draw his attention to any sudden movements.

Muldoon shouted something that sounded like "Vil-check!" and the goalie turned around again. Ari remembered seeing the name Vlcek on the roster and assumed she'd just learned how to correctly pronounce it. "Keep your head in the game."

"Sorry, coach."

One of the white jerseys fired a puck at the net. Vlcek dropped down onto one knee and deflected it. Muldoon whooped and applauded the save.

Ari counted the men on the ice and the rest lined up on the bench. They all seemed present and accounted for, so she crept away from the wall and went back downstairs. She put her disguise back on before she reached the ground floor. Now that she knew where the benches were, she could guess about the location of locker rooms. She quickly made her way around to the front of the building and peeked through doors until she found the right one.

The reek of maleness hit her across the face as soon as the door was open. Actually going into the fog of it nearly toppled her. She forced herself to ignore it even as her eyes started watering. Her wolf senses were sometimes a great asset, but times like this could turn them into a curse very quickly. The damn thing wasn't even officially in use yet, but the two dozen bags and street clothes hanging in the cubbies had already turned the atmosphere toxic.

She powered through the reek, blinking away the tears in her eyes as she searched through the bag closest to the door. Clothes and deodorant, keys, wallet with an ID for Gladstone. She moved on to the next one. She didn't know exactly what she was looking for but hoped it would present itself quickly. She found Aulie's bag and took special care when she went through it. She found a Dopp kit filled with his toiletries and unzipped it. Sitting right on top of everything was a box of Trojans. She wondered what kind of man needed to keep a box of condoms in his gym bag. Was he really in danger of having that much unexpected sex?

At the bottom of the kit she found a Tylenol bottle. She would have dismissed it, but her mind flashed to a story Dale once told her. Her mother had kept M&Ms in pill bottles so Dale wouldn't sneak them. With the diabolical Mrs. Frye in mind, Ari twisted off the cap and peered inside. She had popped enough Tylenol when her transformations caused anguish that she immediately knew it was something else in the bottle. She tapped one of the small flat capsules into her palm and used her phone to take a picture. After a moment of consideration, she took out an evidence bag and slipped the pill inside instead of returning it to the bottle.

She had just put Aulie's bag back when she heard the clatter of someone coming down the ramp in full hockey gear. She only had time to count her blessings that it was only one player instead of the whole team before the goalie, Roman Vlcek, came around the corner. He had thick black hair that had been mashed down to his skull by the helmet that was now under his arm, but it feathered out closer to his neck. His nose was so flat that his eyes seemed oddly far apart. His entire face looked flat, in fact, and rounded at the sides to make him look like a LEGO toy. He stopped when he saw her.

"Who're you?"

He had an accent she couldn't place, and she didn't remember where Dale's research had said he was from. She hoped the language barrier went both ways. "I'm-a, you know," she gestured vaguely toward the door, "with the company, the guys, you know."

"Oh," he said.

"I'll get out of your way."

Vlcek moved toward the locker as Ari retreated toward the

door. Their paths brought them within sniffing distance of each other just long enough for the hairs on the back of Ari's neck to stand up. It wasn't necessarily picking up a scent or anything as tangible as that; she simply felt something when they got closer to each other. He felt it too, pulling back and straightening up so he could face her more fully. They stared at each other and processed the information they'd just received.

"Wolf?" Vlcek said under his breath.

Ari nodded slowly. "You?"

"*Da.* Yes." He looked toward the doorway leading back out to the ice and kept his voice low. "Are there many of us here? I hoped, but I hadn't seen much. There was the thing with the hunters..."

"There are a fair amount, yeah." She followed his gaze back to the door. She didn't want anyone involved with the hit-and-run to come in and see her snooping around. "I should probably get out of here before the rest of the team shows up. There's a bar in Seattle. Bull and Terrier. They know me there. It's a *canidae* bar, lets in all kinds."

He said, "I appreciate that. What's your name?"

She considered giving an alias. "Ariadne. It would probably be best if you didn't mention this to the other guys."

"Why?"

"Just... a feeling."

He shrugged and said, "Okay. It was good to meet you, though. I'm Roman."

She shook his hand before she left. She was still close enough to hear the other players talking when they entered the locker room. The fresh air of the hallway was a godsend after the locker room fug. On her way out of the building, someone else with a hard hat crossed her path going the other way.

"You with Pettit's crew?"

"Yeah," she said without hesitation.

"Find Watkins and tell him to get his ass upstairs, will ya?"

She nodded and kept walking. Outside, she took off the borrowed hard hat and belt. A man was climbing out of a nearby truck as she headed out of the parking lot.

"Where you going?"

"I gotta go light a fire under Watkins' ass."

He scoffed and shook his head. "Good luck with that."

She shook her head, dismayed at the task ahead of her as she left the arena behind and walked back to where she'd left her car.

She decided that following Oesterle had gotten her this far so she might as well stick with him. She drove to where she could see him when he left the arena and took out the pill so she could examine it while she waited. The mark etched in its face didn't tell her anything: a wide V over a half-circle. It looked like a smiling emoji with angry eyebrows. She sent the pill's picture to Dale and then called her.

"Know anyone who could ID that for us?"

"Maybe. Depends. How mature can you be?"

Ari said, "Farts."

"Ha-ha. I know someone who works as a pharmaceutical rep. But we sort of used to date."

"Diane and I used to date, and you hang out with her all the time. I can work with someone who has seen your boobies."

Dale laughed despite herself. "I'll give her a call. Are you sure you don't want to take it to the police? Let their lab figure out what it is?"

Ari said, "I thought about that. But if it turns out to be something innocent and word gets around that the police tested an unknown pill from a Totems player's bag..."

"Right. Okay. I'll let you know what Joyce says."

"Joyce?" Ari said. "What, did you date someone's grandma?"

Dale said, "Down, girl. Remind me again, how did you and Diana meet...?"

"Oh right."

"Right," Dale said. "So you better be good."

Ari growled. "I'll try. I did find out something about one of the Totems you won't find online. Vlcek, the goalie? He's... one of us."

"Another one?"

It took her a second to realize Dale thought she meant he was gay. "No. Us as in me and my mother and..."

"Oh. Oh! Wow. That's a pretty big discovery."

"Yeah. Hopefully he won't end up being involved with whatever Muldoon and his guys are doing. Anyway... we'll talk more when I get back. Love you."

"I love you, too."

Ari hung up and held the baggie up to the light, pondering what the pill would do once ingested. Hopefully Dale's ex would be able to provide answers.

Dale texted when she was following Oesterle back into the city.

"Joyce is off today. You can swing by and see if she recognizes the pill." She included the address. When Ari got to a point where she could safely text back, she said she would drop by if Oesterle didn't wind up anywhere illuminating. She followed him through downtown to Sport Restaurant & Bar. She didn't see any reason to hang around, although she could smell the chicken jambalaya even without slowing the car, and decided to take the pill to the expert.

She drove to the building Dale had texted her and found the right apartment. She'd never met a young woman named Joyce, but she still half-expected a blue-hair in a cardigan when the door opened. What she didn't expect was a gangly black woman in a T-shirt that said KIM & KIM in pink lettering. The ampersand was a stylized guitar with a gun for the neck. She was barefoot, and her leggings had a hole in the knee. Her hair was pinned up on top of her head with a chopstick through it.

"The famous Ariadne. Dale said you were coming by." She held out her hand. "Joyce. It's great to finally meet you."

"You too."

Joyce stepped back to let Ari in. "Sorry about the mess. I'm heading to New Zealand next month and it's hectic. Dale said you had a pill you wanted me to identify?"

"Yeah." Ari took the baggie from her pocket. "I can't really tell you much about where it came from or what the case is--"

"That's fine." Joyce held the baggie up and smoothed the plastic out over the pill. "Can you hand me those glasses over there?"

Ari found the black-rimmed glasses and handed them over. "You're not exactly what I expected. Your job, your name..."

Joyce grinned. "Expecting a granny? I get that a lot. I think it's worked in my favor mostly. Joyce King looks real professional on a resume. You, though. You're exactly what I expected."

Ari looked down at her clothes. Jeans and a button-down shirt undone enough to reveal the plain white T-shirt underneath. It had helped her blend in as a fake construction worker, but she was surprised to find it was representative of her as a whole.

"This is what you pictured? A slacker on laundry day?"

"Well," Joyce said, "something like that. I wasn't talking about your outfit, though. Mostly the eyes and the bone structure. You look kind of wild, not to be messed with. Dale was always talking about what a badass you were. Helping out the little guy, saving the day. Did you really take down a ring of jewelry thieves?"

"It was really just three people," Ari said.

"More jewel thieves than I've ever taken down." She gestured at her laptop. "I don't recognize it right off. I can look at our catalogue online and see if there's anything similar."

Ari followed her to the desk. "I'd appreciate that."

"No sweat." She scooted her chair closer to the desk. "So you and Dale are together now?"

"Yeah. Couple of years."

"That's cool." She was tying as she spoke, scanning row upon row of pills before Ari could register any particular one. "We only broke up because I kept wanting to go on crazy adventures. Like New Zealand. The thing that finally made us call it quits was Bolivia. Who doesn't want to go cave-diving in Bolivia? But she couldn't..." She laughed and looked at Ari. "I guess that makes sense now. Every time I suggested going on a vacation, she said she couldn't leave work for that long. She didn't want to leave you in the lurch."

Ari said, "Sorry..."

"Oh, don't be. I think she really did care about her job that much. And she never seemed too keen on the thrill-seeking. We weren't meant to be. I wish the two of you all the best. Dale deserves it."

Ari smiled. "Yeah, she does."

Joyce scrolled down, then back up, and snapped her fingers. "There you go. Cynosylline."

"How the hell do these things get their names?"

"More commonly called Cyn. It's a nootropic... a 'smart' drug that's supposed to increase your awareness and cognition. My company doesn't offer it and... wow, it's actually banned in America. It was mixed with... uh..." She looked at Ari over her glasses. "I'm going to dumb this down for you. No offense."

"None taken. You lost me at nootropic."

"Okay, so it helps people focus. But it's mixed with other stuff that keeps users awake, gives them more energy and stamina. It's like an amphetamine mixed with caffeine with a Five Hour Energy used as the base."

Ari had looked at the screen to write down the pill's name. "Wow, no wonder the FDA doesn't like it. It's safe to say this drug would be on a sports team's no-no list, right?"

Joyce leaned back and waved her hand at the screen. "Any sport, any league, would go ape shit if a player tested positive for this stuff."

And there was the smoking gun. She took the baggie back and Joyce escorted her back to the door. "Thank you, Joyce. This was extremely helpful."

"Sure. It's not every day I get to help a private eye with a case. And I understand this is all hush-hush. My lips are sealed."

"I appreciate it." She gestured at the T-shirt. "Band?"

"Comic book. Great comic book. Dale would love it."

"I'll remember to tell her about it. Good luck in New Zealand."

Joyce nodded and offered her hand. "If you ever need any other pharmaceutical help, you know who to call."

"Will do."

She left the apartment and transferred the written pill name to her phone. From what Joyce had said, it sounded like Cyn was a kind of super-steroid. If four players were using the drug, she could definitely see Halphen going to desperate measures and then admitting to attempted murder to protect everyone else. The team could be devastated by the bad press before they even played a single game, but the more pressing concern was that Muldoon and all the players he supplied could be looking at serious jail time.

She had to be extremely careful about how she proceeded or else she might find out just how far Muldoon was willing to go in order to keep the secret.

Chapter Twelve

Dale was already reading in bed when Ari got out of the shower. "It's not as much fun without you. When did the doctor say you would be back in action?"

"Couple of weeks. Sorry, puppy."

"That's okay. I don't mind being on top."

Dale smirked at her as she walked around the foot of the bed. "Are you sure you don't want to take that pill to someone? Now that we know how staggeringly illegal it is, I don't really feel comfortable keeping it in the office."

"It's safe. All the security Cecily forced on us made sure we'll know if anyone tries to get to it." Ari sat on the edge of the bed to rub lotion onto her legs. "I could take the pill to Wiseman, tell him that I think those four players are using it, and get them kicked off the team. But what if those are just the four I happened to see? What if the whole team is using this junk? Or what if Aulie is the only one? I need to be sure this is the smoking gun we think it is before I pull the trigger."

Dale said, "You don't pull the trigger on a smoking gun."

"You know what I mean. Right now I can only nail Aulie with the pill. I could let Diana know and she could arrest him. But I want to get the source."

"Come up here."

Ari twisted and put her feet on the pillow. Dale put her book down and started massaging the lotion into Ari's legs for her. "Muldoon is probably the source."

"I'll go with that theory." Ari put her hands behind her head. "So Muldoon gets the pills..."

Dale snapped her fingers. "And they have the exchange at the Newton Ice Rink! That's why they're going there instead of the Tukwila facility."

Ari said, "That makes sense. It's a lot less public than doing it at their official rink, plus if anyone asks what they're doing there, he can just claim they're practicing on different ice for away games. He puts the drugs in their lockers, they pick it up, and they never actually pass it between themselves. No one can catch the coach giving his players illegal drugs. Halphen... he's the muscle. Muldoon finds out I'm sniffing around and sends his goon out to take care of me."

"Like the enforcer."

"Right. God, I hope Dubov isn't involved in this shit. He's got enough going on without a drug charge to deal with."

Dale moved down to Ari's feet. "The manager of the marina called while you were out."

Ari lifted her head. "Was there another vandalism?"

"No, that's the thing. Since there haven't been any more incidents, he feels you might have scared off whoever was doing it. If nothing happens this Sunday, he's going to consider the case closed."

"If he's happy not knowing who did it, then I'm more than happy to get my Sunday nights back. I'm just worried whoever is doing is was scared off seeing me there and, if I leave, they'll just start up again. Call him back, tell him I'll be in Friday to pick up the final check. Then on Sunday, I'll go back as the wolf and see if anyone shows up."

"I'll call him in the morning." She patted the bottom of Ari's foot. "Turn around."

Ari tickled Dale's foot. "You sure? It would be a shame to waste this arrangement."

Dale grinned. "Sorry, puppy. Another night."

Ari twisted around and got under the blankets. Dale turned off the lamp and let Ari pull her close. She was wearing a tank top, and Ari traced circles on the bare skin around one strap.

"How did you meet Joyce?"

"I thought you weren't jealous," Dale murmured.

"I'm not. I was just thinking about her interests. World traveling and spelunking in Bolivia. It kind of made me curious if that part of the appeal."

Dale repositioned her head on Ari's shoulder. "Sure. It means she was very athletic and liked adventure. But I'm too much of a homebody to travel all over the world. Not to mention the fact she can barely afford those trips. She had a huge amount of debt because of plane tickets, hotels, buying gear. It was the main thing that made me break up with her."

Ari stroked her back. "So with me... you get adventure, but you also get to sleep in your own bed every night."

"Our bed."

"Right." She kissed Dale's hair. "Our bed. I'm sorry I tried to protect you. It won't happen again. And I promise, I'm going to keep Bitches up and running for as long as you want to work there."

Dale lifted her head and kissed Ari's chin, then her lips. "Can't beat that job security."

Ari smiled and guided Dale's head back down to her chest. She wasn't going to shutter Bitches just to keep Dale safe, but she was going to do everything in her power to make sure Dale wasn't touched by danger any more than necessary.

Sunday night, officially the last night of the vandalism case, Ari had Dale drive her to a park a few blocks east of the marina. Ari wasn't sure it was a good idea for her to drive with her injured ankle, but Dale insisted she could handle a quick and easy drive. It was just before dusk and still light enough out that they took a second to make sure the park was empty before Ari climbed into the backseat. The sky was scarlet, gold, and banded with purple reflected in the lake's water. Even with the hum of traffic on the interstate, it was easy to get lost in the beauty of nature.

Dale kept an eye out while Ari stripped in the backseat. "I used to dream about this, you know." She met Ari's eye in the rearview mirror. "Hot chick stripping down in the backseat. The difference is that usually I was stripping down, too."

"We have some time before it gets dark. Want to neck a little?"

Dale chuckled. "This is work time, puppy. Focus."

"Right. I'm going to spend the whole night out here, just in case they decide to hit before dawn. If they show up before then, I'll get to the stash we hid and change back if it's safe. If it's not, I'll just observe so I can confront them later on."

Dale nodded. She knew all of this, but Ari knew that having the details laid out would help keep her calm. She was going to be safe at home while Ari was out in the elements, alone and without backup.

She settled against the back seat and tucked her arms in close to her chest. The wolf was there, as always, hiding at the back of her senses and waiting for her to give the go-ahead to take over. When she felt her body beginning to change she opened her eyes and lay down. It was easier to transform while lying down; it took the weight off her extremities and gave them a chance to reposition more naturally. She stretched her neck out as her shoulders collapsed and her ribs pushed out.

When it was over she flipped onto her forepaws and shook out her fur. Dale twisted in her seat and cupped Ari's face, kissing the now sloped plane of her forehead.

"All good?"

Ari licked her face and Dale laughed. She opened the back door to let Ari out. "Be safe, puppy. Only change back if you're absolutely certain it's safe. Otherwise I'll be back here at the crack of dawn to pick you up."

Ari huffed her acknowledgement and headed through the park. Spending the night as the wolf would have the added bonus of settling her mind, giving her a chance to work through the details of the Totems case from a new angle. The wolf was steering the ship, all of her animal instincts pushed to the forefront, while her analytical mind could focus on minutiae and the finer details of everything she'd learned.

The past few days she'd rotated between various Totems players to see if any of them went back to the Newton Ice Rink or met up with anyone else suspicious. Oesterle seemed to have two girlfriends, something she put in the file for Wiseman as a potential strike against his character if the drug thing didn't pan out. She followed Lindholm all the way to Anacortes and then rode the ferry with him to discover he had a boat which he kept docked on one of the small islands dotting the Georgia Strait.

Aulie barely left his apartment except to get food and go to the gym. She disguised herself as a janitor and checked out his locker while he was in the sauna. No drugs. And she spent a stunningly busy Saturday following Oborin and his girlfriend through boutiques, chic clothing stores, and fancy restaurants. He flashed his credit card so often that Ari practically had the number memorized.

But other than two-timing, sloth, and what had to be a staggering amount of debt, none of the Newton Five went anywhere near the ice rink and she never saw any drugs exchanged. She tried to surveil Muldoon's home, but there were very few places on his street where she could be inconspicuous, and it seemed like the kind of neighborhood that would call the cops if anyone lingered for too long. Even the wolf wasn't a good alternative, since she was sure the Homeowner's Association would have Animal Control on her faster than lightning. She would have to find another way to tail him if she wanted to know where the drugs were coming from.

She arrived at the apartment building that faced the marina. A few sailors were still hanging around, mooring their boats and finishing conversations on the docks. Ari found a spot next to a minivan and hunkered down to wait until the parking lot was empty. Darkness crept across the sky and the security lights flickered on. People said their goodbyes, voices echoing off the water and bouncing back to Ari, and soon the parking lot was empty.

Why only Sunday? The vandals only struck on Sunday night, so what was the significance? They didn't seem to be targeting anyone in particular, other than the marina itself, so why not on Wednesday night when it would be more likely deserted?

Her ears twitched at every passing car, and occasionally a jogger passed by, but none of them ever slowed. She had to fight to stay awake and eventually got up to pace the length of the apartment building. Something smelled delicious in the dumpster, but she forced herself to ignore it. She didn't want to spend the morning nauseated when whatever the wolf considered gourmet left a rotten taste in her human mouth.

A few yards to the south, separated from the marina by a stretch of water, was a bank of houseboats. The majority of the windows were lit, though blocked by curtains. Occasionally someone would come out to look across the lake or to have a beer under the stars. Ari saw one pair of men engage in a quick and seemingly illicit tryst before sneaking back inside. The lights started extinguishing around ten o'clock, until around midnight when only a few outliers remained.

She didn't know exactly what time it was when a guy came out onto his back deck and lit up a cigarette. She noticed him because he seemed to be focused on the marina. "C'mere," he called over his shoulder, just loud enough to carry through the quiet of the night. Another man came out of the house and joined him. Smoker pointed at the marina. Smoker's Friend leaned to one side and shook his head. After a long moment, Smoker tossed his cigarette into the water and they both went inside.

A few minutes later, the two men appeared on the road. Smoker had pulled a hoodie up over his curly hair, while Smoker's Friend had on a baseball cap. Smoker was carrying a duffel bag tucked against his side. When they reached the marina they slowed and scanned the parking lot. Ari felt vindicated but also frustrated at herself. Every night she'd wasted sitting and staring while the guys she was waiting for watched from their houseboat.

Convinced there was no one watching, they crossed onto the property and quickly scaled the chain-link security fence. Ari got to her feet and moved forward in a crouch. The fence rattled when the vandals jumped off onto the other side. She listened to their footsteps on the dock and followed them, squeezing between the wall and the gate. The sound of spray paint cans being shaken led her straight to the two men.

She assumed an attack stance, lowered her head, and bellowed out her loudest bark. Smoker nearly jumped out of his sneakers. His friend spun around and hurled his spray can at her. She ducked to one side and it bounced uselessly off the dock, rolling until she heard the splash when it fell into the water. Ari barked again, trying to be as intimidating as possible, baring her teeth and thrashing her head from side to side.

"Damn dog!" Smoker yelled.

"Let's get the hell out of here before he attacks." His friend ran off before seeing if Smoker was following.

Smoker bent his knees and swayed from side to side. Ari lunged at him, hoping to make him run as well. She could follow them straight back to their apartment and give the marina owner and police an exact address. He feinted with his right hand then juked to the left, bringing him closer to the lake than an exit. Ari pursued and snapped at his feet. He twisted at the waist and she heard a loud hiss right next to her ear. She recoiled as something wet rained down on her. Spray paint coated the top of her head and down the back of her neck. In the seconds she was distracted, Smoker smacked her on top of the head with the can, then stepped around her and made a break for the fence.

Ari gave chase, thoroughly pissed off now. Smoker cleared the fence in a single leap and fumbled over the other side, hitting the ground on all fours and scrambling to his feet. Ari pushed herself through the gap again. Smoker kicked at her and she closed her jaws around his ankle. He shrieked and kicked her off. She twisted away just before his sneaker connected with her snout. She remembered that he had to get away in order for her to get his address, so she backed off. He got up, grabbed his duffel bag, and fled. She let him get a good head-start and then ran after him.

It was difficult letting him stay ahead of her. He was slow and kept looking back to see if she was gaining. Fortunately, they didn't have far to go. Smoker turned and ran along the wooden dock that connected all the houseboats. His friend was on the porch of their house and motioned for him to hurry.

"It's right behind you, dude!"

"I know, asshole! Get the BB gun!"

That almost stopped Ari short, but she had to lock down the address. Smoker and his friend went inside and Ari put on a burst of speed. She looked at the house number, illuminated by their porchlight, and skidded to a stop as the men came back outside.

"Just wing it," Smoker's Friend said.

"Fuck that, thing tried to bite my foot off. I'm gonna blind the son of a bitch."

Ari could possibly have outrun the gun, but she didn't want to risk it. She hated the water, despised and feared the idea of going for a swim, but at the moment it was the lesser evil. Instead of fleeing back to land, she cut left. She heard the "pfft!" of the rifle as she was already airborne.

"Oh, shit!"

She hit the water smoothly, slipping under the surface like a dart. Panic rushed through her but she ignored it as she turned herself toward shore. Parts of her mind flashed with warnings that she was underwater, just in case it had slipped her notice, but she ignored them all. She paddled her feet, keeping her head below water just in case Smoker was still on his mission to blind her. When she reached the shore she chanced a look back. Smoker and his friend had already gone back inside.

Shivering and fighting a bit of shock at what she'd just done, she went directly to the stash she and Dale had left earlier. She picked it up with her teeth and went to a public restroom nearby. Homeless people sometimes used it to clean up, and she figured she could do the same thing. She made sure the women's side was empty, went into a stall, and transformed.

The trauma of her swim hit her hard. She leaned against the partition and hugged herself, shuddering violently as she tried and failed to keep from crying. She'd thought her phobia was under control after her last unexpected submersion, but apparently it was still lingering.

Once the worst of the shaking passed, she took her clothes from the bag and dressed herself in jeans and a faded Sesame Street T-shirt. It had been ages since she'd woken Dale up in the middle of the night for a ride home. Dale might actually appreciate the nostalgia of it. All she knew for certain was that she didn't want to transform again when her emotions were so fraught.

She left the stall and went to the sink to splash water on her face. She twisted the faucets, glanced at her reflection, and froze. The entire right side of her face was bright blue. The only part that had been spared was the lower right-hand quadrant of her jaw and cheekbone. She lifted her hair and saw that the spray paint was indeed still on the skin there as well. In all the excitement of the chase and her traumatizing escape, she'd forgotten all about Smoker spraying her. She rested her hands on the sink and hung her newly-blue head.

"Well, shit."

CHAPTER THIRTEEN

DALE'S FIRST instinct was to laugh until she saw the look in Ari's eyes. Ari explained what happened on the drive home and Dale comforted her as best she could while driving. When they got home, Dale managed to support Ari while also limping along with her crutch. She turned on the lights and guided Ari into the bathroom. She didn't question why she was so shaken by what happened; she had a thing about heights and knew she would've felt the same way if someone dangled her off the top of the Space Needle. She shuddered just thinking about it.

Dale folded a towel on the sink and patted it. Ari hopped up and Dale went back to the kitchen. She came back with a bottle of olive oil, took a bag of cotton balls from behind the mirror, and wet one of them down.

"You look like you've done this before."

"Well, never off anyone's face." She began to dab the cotton ball to Ari's cheek. "I had a few run-ins with spray paint during high school."

Ari smiled. "You were a vandal?"

"Oh, no. No, not a vandal. Just a bored kid in the middle of nowhere Pennsylvania. There were a lot of boarded-up buildings that needed the Dale Frye touch. I usually wore gloves, but some of the people I ran with didn't have the same foresight."

"Any girls?"

The corners of Dale's mouth twitched. "Maybe..."

"Little baby-gay Dale, tenderly cleaning the paint off the homecoming queen's hands..."

Dale laughed. "The homecoming queen had no idea I existed."

Ari said, "Her loss."

Dale exchanged the cotton ball for a fresh one. "Do you want to talk about what happened?"

"Not really."

"Okay."

Ari let herself be cleaned for a full minute, eyes closed so Dale could wipe around them. "I thought I was over it. When I got tossed off the boat a last year, I thought... okay, my phobia has been realized, so I can get past it now."

Dale said, "Maybe you did get a little past it. I mean, you were thrown into the water and survived. That was enough to give you the courage to jump when your life depended on it. It just means you can't turn off fear like flipping a switch."

"Maybe not. Tell me more about washing girl's hands when you were a teenager."

"It never went beyond rubbing baby oil on their fingers."

Ari coughed.

"You know what I mean. But that was probably the first time I ever touched anyone that way. Holding their hands, cleaning their nails for them... it was very intimate." She dragged the cotton ball over the curve of Ari's cheek, sweeping away a bit of blue shade. "It's a wonder I didn't become a manicurist."

"I wish I had blocked my face with my hands, then."

"You should have. This could've been toxic. It could have choked you, blinded you, done any number of horrible things to you far worse than the BB gun."

Ari said, "I know."

Dale pressed her lips together in a firm line. "I get it. Wanting to protect me by taking the GG&M job. I feel the same way on nights like this. So I'm not mad at you for considering the offer. I would have considered it, too."

"Good." She took a cotton ball of her own and began wiping another section of her face.

"Do you think when you transform back into the wolf, you'll still have paint in your fur?"

"I doubt it. The paint transferred to my skin when I

transformed, so taking it off… I mean, it would be like the paint spontaneously reappearing when I wolf out."

Dale wrinkled her brow. "So… where does it go? The fur. Does it retract into your body or… I know some of it is your hair. Right? It's… the same follicles…"

"I don't know."

"How could you not know?"

Ari shrugged. "Point at your gallbladder."

"I… what?" She looked down at her torso. "It's… here? Right?"

Ari said, "I don't have a clue. Just because I can transform into a wolf doesn't mean I know absolutely everything about the process. Is there another layer of skin just under this where the pelt comes from? Or does the hair actually grow and then retract? Dunno. Why do I weigh less when I'm the wolf? That shouldn't be possible. Where does the extra mass go? What the hell is my dental situation?" She shrugged again. "It's just who I am and what I can do. There are *canidae* like Dr. Frost who have a better grasp on the hows and whys of it, but I personally don't know."

"I would be so curious about it."

"Maybe I'll try to learn more." She opened one eye. "How's it looking?"

Dale winced and stepped back. A small pile of blue cotton balls had grown next to the sink while they were talking. "A little less like you're freezing to death. It might take a few more passes before you're back to normal."

"Sorry. This is more sleep deprivation than you're used to."

"But not more than I'm willing to suffer. I'll just call my boss and tell her I'll be late tomorrow. Don't smile, I'm working on that part of your cheek."

Ari tried to keep her face still. "I was hoping this job would give me a chance to think about the Totems case."

"Any insights?"

"Nothing worth noting. I still have to catch someone in the act. Lindholm has a boat. It could be like what Wayne Corbett had going on the island. Pick up drugs from Canada, bring them in across the water. I could follow that trail a little further and see what I find out."

Dale put oil on another cotton ball and brushed it along the line of Ari's jaw. "Be careful when you do. And if you can't be careful, then know I'm waiting to take care of you."

Ari squeezed Dale's hand. Maybe the dangers of their job didn't matter so long as they could keep that in mind. She might get shot at, beaten up, thrown into the water, or any number of other threats, but she knew Dale would always be there to pick up the pieces and patch her up. And she would be there for Dale when she brought the danger to their doorstep. For now, that would be enough.

In the morning, Ari wrote her report about what she'd seen and where the vandals had gone. She had to invent a story about a guard dog she'd hired to help her out. She hated to lie on an official report, but it was second nature to her now. She couldn't very well explain that she had been the dog, that she'd been the one pursuing the vandals back home, without having her credibility and sanity questioned. They referred to the wolf as "Tule" in all official documents, just in case any judge or lawyer demanded she be presented as a witness.

Dale checked her face in the sunlight to make sure they'd gotten off as much of the spray paint as possible. There was still a bit of blue on her ears and jaw, but makeup covered it enough for her to be out in public. She didn't like wearing that much makeup, but it was preferable to looking as if she was bruised on the cheek and throat.

When the report was ready, she went to the marina and reported her findings in person to the owner. He listened and, when she got to the part about where the culprits lived, he went to the window and leaned out to look toward them. He pointed.

"That one there?"

"That would be it, sir, yes."

He cursed under his breath. "That's why it was always on Sunday. Un-damn-believable, those little bastards." He walked back to his desk and heaved himself into his seat. "It was happening on Sunday so it would be the first thing I had to deal with Monday morning. I'm going to kill those assholes."

Ari thought about asking for more details, but it really wasn't any of her business. She had been hired to find out who was vandalizing the marina and its boats. She'd done that, and now the owner was writing her a check, and that meant her involvement was officially over. She accepted the check, thanked him, and went back to the office where Dale could officially close the case in their files.

While Dale dealt with the paperwork, Ari investigated the black market for Cynosylline. Newspaper reports indicated there was a pretty steady flow of the drug up from Mexico and through the San Diego port. A quick side trip onto Conor Muldoon's website revealed he spent two seasons coaching a team in Phoenix, Arizona. The Mexican border was practically in his backyard and San Diego was just a decent-sized road trip away.

She sent Diana a text, asking her to call when she had a few minutes to spare. Her phone rang less than a minute after she sent the message.

"This really is something that could wait," Ari said when she picked up.

"I took the day off. Lucy had an appointment and I wanted to spend some time with her. But anything that breaks up the monotony of daytime TV is a godsend. I mean, god, how many game shows *are* there?"

Ari smiled. "How is Lucy doing?"

"As well as can be expected, I guess. A day at a time. But come on, I've been thinking about this nonstop. Give me some escapism."

"Sorry, I was just calling for a recommendation. Do you know anyone on the drug... squad? The drug unit?"

"Narcotics?"

"That's the word."

Diana said, "Yeah, I know some people over there. I could put in a good word if you need me to. What have you gotten yourself into this time?"

"Can't say. I just need to know how someone might hypothetically get their hands on a drug."

"Uh-huh." Ari could hear her moving on the other end of the line. "Do you have a pen?"

Ari said, "I'm sitting at a computer. I can type it in."

"Wow, futuristic. Okay, Sophie Lehman is an undercover detective. I can find out where she is and get you a meeting with her. Give me an hour or so."

"Thanks, Diana."

It only took forty-five minutes for another text to arrive. "Zanjeer, the Indian restaurant outside the Northgate Mall. One hour. She'll be in a baseball cap. Dress to depress."

Ari smiled and went to check the small wardrobe to see what clothes she had in the hopes she wouldn't have to go all the way home. She found a faded plaid shirt that was worn down at the elbows and a jacket with a broken zipper. She tucked her hair under a beanie and looked in the mirror to see if she looked "junkie" enough to meet with an undercover narcotics detective. Dale stopped her before she left the office and volunteered her emergency pair of eyeglasses, the ones with the thick pink frames.

"Junkies have bad eyesight?" Ari asked, blinking through the lenses.

"I don't know… it just seems to complete the outfit. But at the very least they take some of the attention off how pretty you are."

Ari kissed her cheek. "Flirt. I'll bring you something sweet when I come back."

Traffic slowed her progress to Northgate but she managed to arrive without too much delay. Sophie Lehman was sitting at the back booth, baseball cap twisted backward, hands crossed at the wrist and her fingers tapping a beat on the tabletop. She looked up as Ari approached.

"You D's friend?"

"Yeah. You the lady I'm supposed to be meeting?"

She gestured at the booth across from her and Ari took a seat. "Call me Mirth if you have to call me anything. Last name is supposed to be Murphy, meth-heads missing too many teeth to get it right, so…" She flipped her fingers in a 'what are you gonna do' gesture. "Who are you?"

Ari wasn't sure if she needed a cover. "Tule. I was hoping you could give me some information. Drug called Cynosylline."

Sophie kept her head turned toward the window and her eyes moving, following traffic outside the restaurant instead of looking at Ari. "Street name is Cyn, sometimes Sweet Cyn. Supposed to give you hyper-focus and tons of stamina. People call it Five-Hundred Hour Energy. The downside is that it causes dependency to a scary degree. You stop taking it, you crash like the Hindenburg. One kid in… uh… somewhere in the east. Detroit, Chicago, Cleveland, ended up in a coma when his supply ran out. Plus, whoever created it mixed in a lot of shit that leads to a whole laundry list of side effects. Insomnia, depression, high blood pressure, anxiety, memory loss."

"Yeah, but hyper-focus and stamina. Sports teams must love it."

Sophie shook her head. "You'd think so, but no. Stuff turns up on a drug test like a thunderstorm on a radar screen."

Ari was stumped by that, but she let it slide. "You seem pretty educated on it."

"I try to be educated on everything I might run into out here." The waitress approached and filled a coffee cup for Ari. Sophie remained silent until she was gone. "What's your interest?"

"I think someone is bringing it into Seattle. Not to distribute. Well, not beyond a small group of friends and users. I want to know where he's getting it, see if I can find out how much he's getting and maybe cut off his supply."

Sophie pushed her lips out and narrowed her eyes as she considered it. "Cyn gets the most traffic by the University, for the obvious reasons. I haven't heard of anyone getting busted for selling recently, though. Students are already broke enough without adding a designer-drug habit on top of it all."

"Cyn's expensive?"

"Thirty pills run you three bills."

Ari whistled. "Three hundred?"

"Three thousand. Like I said, this thing... you hear about that drug last year? Wolfsbane?"

"Uh, yeah, I think I heard something about it."

Sophie said, "That garbage was entirely synthetic, crafted in a lab for maximum effect. It was expensive as hell, too. I never even once saw a hint of it in real life."

Ari wished she had been so lucky.

"Cyn is the same thing. Lots of hype if you're listening in the right places, but your standard drug user is going to find something cheaper. The person you think is handing it out to his pals. Is he rich?"

"Yeah, he's pretty well off."

"Then at some point, he's probably sold the shit. I can ask around, see if anyone has heard about a new influx. Angle I'm working now, it would make sense I want to score a wake-up pill."

Ari said, "I appreciate it." She wrote down her number on a napkin and passed it to Sophie instead of offering a card. "Thanks for your help."

"Any friend of D."

She started to reach for her wallet, but Ari waved her off. The meeting was her idea, so coffee was her treat. Sophie left and Ari watched through the window as she walked away. Muldoon was doping his boys with a drug that would eventually leave them dependent on his supply. She'd started out looking for ways to take them down for the drug, but now she could see that the players might just be victims of their coach.

Either way, she needed to get Muldoon out of the way and get the players help before it was too late.

CHAPTER FOURTEEN

DALE'S PHONE was on speaker, propped against her coffee cup to amplify the sound of Ari's voice. She'd made sure Ari was using the hands-free hookup before letting the conversation begin. She listened to what Ari had learned about Cyn and its side effects, then turned to face her computer and began typing.

"Are you on your way back to the office?"

"I was going to make another stop first. There's someone I need to talk to."

Dale said, "Okay. Hopefully I'll have something for you by the time you get back. Love you."

"I love you," Ari said.

Dale disconnected the phone and focused all her energy on the computer. She had bookmarked most of the Totems players, their histories, all the biographical information that she thought they might need in the course of the investigation. She called up the Muldoon tab and skimmed over it with a new eye. He started his coaching career in Detroit, so she started there. Not a bad record, but no championship. He was with them for two years before he moved to St. Louis. That was the first team he got to the playoffs, so she made a note of the dates and did a side search. After that, Muldoon spent a long stretch in Phoenix. She did a second side search on that city.

An hour later, she called Ari. "Hey, where are you?"

"The waterfront. I'm waiting for the guy I wanted to talk with. What's up?"

"I was thinking about what you were told about Cyn's side effects. Mainly the withdrawals leading to depression and comas. I started looking at the cities he left behind in his career. Now, Muldoon has never been touched by scandals. But that's because he's always long gone by the time the problems show up. He's like a shady contractor who puts on a shitty roof and hightails it to Montana before the next storm comes along.

"I found two former hockey players in Detroit who wound up in the hospital six and ten months after Muldoon moved to Phoenix. One had fallen into a coma. He never woke up from it. The other one tried to commit suicide. He was managed to succeed at killing himself two years later. His family said he'd become depressed after leaving the team. Now, I mean, that's a valid reason for someone to be depressed, but knowing what we know..."

"Sounds like Cyn might have been involved. Was there anything in Phoenix?"

"Another player suicide. His wife said he was suffering from insomnia and anxiety."

Ari said, "Fits the bill."

"I thought so. I can keep digging to see if anyone else shows up."

"Do it. I'll put it together in a file for GG&M when I drop the bombshell they're officially going to need a new coach. I don't know what I'd do without you, Dale."

"With any luck you won't have to find out. Good luck with your meeting."

"Thanks. Hopefully he won't keep me waiting. I'll call you when I'm on the way back."

"Be safe."

She hung up again and sighed. If anyone could protect the team, it was Ariadne. She just had to find enough evidence to hang Muldoon and get him away from the players so they could get the help they needed. Dale was more than happy to do her part. She flexed her fingers before she rested them on the keyboard to start searching for more skeletons.

A brief shower had left Waterfront Park's fixtures beaded with raindrops. The boardwalk was soaked under her sneakers but the weather hadn't kept the tourists away. They gathered at the railing to take pictures of ferries pulling across the Sound or to wave at friends and family members riding the Ferris wheel. A few were gathered around the coin-operated telescopes to scan for wildlife.

Ari paused by the statue of Christopher Columbus and took a moment to take in the view. The park was anchored by the aquarium at one end and the Great Wheel at the other. Looking west she could see wide expanses of water broken only by the wake of ferries and the wooded side of Bainbridge Island. Turning around to look east, she could see the towering wall of the Alaskan Way Viaduct humming with the constant flow of traffic. Beyond it were the upper stories of downtown Seattle and tall cranes hanging over it all. She felt well-balanced between the natural and man-made sides of her city and took a moment to breathe in the scent of the water and the just-after-a-rain smell.

This was her city, and this was the life she had built for herself. She wasn't built to sit behind a desk at GG&M, no matter how heavy the paycheck might be.

"You look deep in thought."

She jumped, so caught up that she hadn't heard Dubov approaching. He had his hoodie pulled up over a baseball cap, the upper half of his face hidden by sunglasses. She gestured toward a seating area near the fountain where they could be at least partially unnoticed by passersby. He followed her and they sat next to each other on a bench that faced the water.

"Sorry if I startled you," he said.

"Don't be. I should've been watching for you. Nice outfit."

He smiled. "Bryan called it Unabomber chic. But I thought if I had to meet with you, I might want to look insuspicious."

She assumed he meant inconspicuous and smiled without correcting him. She liked his word better. "I have a problem, Mr. Dubov."

"You can call me Tyler." He shifted uncomfortably and scanned the crowd. They were both keeping their voices down, and the fountain behind them was loud enough to discourage eavesdropping, but she understood his anxiety. "Is it about me coming out? 'Cause I talked to Bryan about it, and I'm going to talk to the coach, and I think I just have to find the right time. I stopped with those awful tweets and–"

Ari said, "It's actually not about that. As long as the tweets have stopped, I don't care when you come out. That's your schedule. I have a problem with the other guys on your team." She took out the baggie with the Cyn pill and put it on her thigh so he could see it without actually passing it over. No good ever came from one person passing another a baggie with a pill in it, especially not when one of those people was obviously hiding his identity. "You recognize that?"

"It's a pill?" He leaned closer. "Uh... no? What's it for?"

"It's called Cyn, Sweet Cyn, Cynosylline... It's a performance-enhancing drug."

Dubov leaned away quickly. "Ah, geez. What are you doing with that?"

"I got it from one of your teammates' bags. You've never seen anyone popping pills like this?"

He shrugged. "Guys pop pills all the time. Caffeine pills, shit for anxiety, pain, whatever. Hell, it's not even just sports. Everybody's popping pills all day long. But I've never, like, examined what they're taking. One of my guys has this?"

"If it helps, it's one of the guys you told me felt sketchy about."

He didn't look comforted.

"What I don't understand is how they're getting away with it. This drug stays in their system long enough to get picked up on a drug test."

Dubov laughed and leaned forward, elbows across his knees. "You know how many guys in the NHL have been caught doping in the last ten years? Three. Out of, what, eight hundred guys on the ice. You look at football and baseball where performance-enhancing drugs are considered a necessary evil, you think hockey is just that clean? No, our screening is a joke. You know how often I've been tested in my entire career? Four times."

Ari said, "So they don't care?"

"They're just not looking. And if they do find someone who tests positive, like the blind squirrel finding an acorn, they just get a twenty-game suspension for the first offense. Most of us are paid well enough that we can deal with that just fine. This stuff's really bad?"

"A guy in Detroit fell into a coma when his supply ran out. He never woke up. Some others suffered from anxiety and depression. Tried to kill themselves. At least one of them was successful."

Dubov hung his head and pushed his hoodie off. "There are guys on my team using it?"

"At least one I know of. Three more I suspect. Could be more than that."

He stood up so suddenly that Ari thought he was lashing out at her. When she realized he was walking away, she got to her feet and pursued.

"Where are you going?"

"I'm going to protect my team, like I'm supposed to. I'm going to kick all their asses until they 'fess up, and then I'm gonna flush these damn pills down the toilet."

Ari put a hand on his arm. "I appreciate that feeling, trust me. But there's a better way to deal with it. The guys who are using this stuff might just be victims the same way the guy in the coma and the players who committed suicide. If you go running in there smashing faces, they might stop, but the person pushing the drugs on them could walk away scot-free. It could just make him smarter about covering his tracks and then the pills are back in the locker room. We need to cut off the snake's head, and I can only do that if I get more information."

He sighed and looked down at his shoes. "And that only works if no one knows you're looking into it."

"Exactly."

"Who is hurting them?"

Ari considered not telling him, but she knew he would figure it out himself given enough time. "Muldoon." His eyes flashed with anger so she put a hand on his chest. "Now hold on. Jumping the gun won't do any good. If what I'm thinking is right, he's gotten away with this for years. He's smart and he's very good at shifting the blame. By the time his players wound up in the hospital, he was long gone to the next town and the next team."

"I hate this. I hate knowing he's poisoning my boys and I'm just supposed to sit on the bench. Please, Ariadne, give me something."

Ari watched a couple posing by the Columbus statue as she thought. "Start a rumor about drug testing. You don't know when, but you heard that the new owners hired a law firm who is doing an independent test outside the NHL regulations. It's a new team, so it makes sense they would be extra-vigilant, right?" He nodded. "It doesn't matter if the tests never happen. The fear might be enough to get the guys to stop using for a couple of days. That's all I'll need. Hopefully."

"I think I can handle that. Okay." He held out his hand. "If you need any help with anything, just let me know."

She took his hand. "I'll do that. Thanks for your help, Tyler."

"No, thank you. I can't repay you for everything you've done for me and Bryan."

"I didn't do anything. Just told you what you already knew."

He nodded and put his hood back up. Ari watched him jog off, gave the Great Wheel one last look, and then went back to where she'd parked. She had an idea. It was insanely risky, and there was a chance someone might call her bluff and her plan would be ended before it began. But she didn't have much of a choice. When she got to her car, she took out her phone and called Wiseman at GG&M. She wanted to keep her promise to Dubov, and that meant not wasting any more time in bring down Muldoon.

Her conversation with Wiseman led to a series of calls between him and the team owner, who finally agreed to play along with Ari's plan. The day after she talked with Dubov on the beach, Ari drove back to the rink in Tukwila and parked in full view in front of the building. She slung a bag over her shoulder, knocked on the door, and someone from the team came to let her in.

The arena seemed abandoned even though it was brand-new. The concession stands lacked signs or lighting, the corridors were cavernous and echoing, and she could hear the clack of hockey sticks on ice like bones in the attic as she went through a pair of double doors and descended to rink-side. She was wearing her beanie and Dale's glasses, but there was still a chance she would be recognized. Her bet was that Muldoon only knew about a private investigator looking into the team and didn't actually know what she looked like. Still, she had done her hair differently under the cap: twin plaits on either side of her head, and she was wearing a pair of shoes she kept in the closet because they affected her gait.Muldoon was standing on the ice with the team. She rocked on the balls of her feet, swaying from side to side instead of standing still. Even people who knew her well might only remember a girl with pigtails and big glasses who seemed overloaded with nervous energy. She waited until the coach noticed her and lifted her hand in greeting. He made his way over to her.

"You the girl? Tule?" He pronounced it like 'tool.'

"Yep." She hunched her shoulder and shot her arm out toward him. "Too-lee. Tule Fletcher."

He gestured at the bag. "Got everything?"

"Picked it up this morning."

Muldoon motioned for her to follow him onto the ice. A carpet stretched from the entrance out to where the team had gathered. Dubov looked up as she approached and narrowed his eyes. She shook her head, disappointed he recognized her so quickly.

She scanned the rest of the team as she approached for signs they could also see through her disguise. Oesterle was talking to Hamilton and Harden. Lindholm was off to one side by himself, both hands resting on top of his stick. Oborin seemed to be showing off his skating skills for Gladstone and Neely. The only member of the Newton Five she didn't see was Aulie. She put down her bag and crouched down to tug open the zipper.

"Okay, boys, gather up. Come on." Muldoon waited for them to settle. "There's someone I'd like you to meet. This is Tool-uh Fletcher. I didn't think we'd be doing it this early, but our owner has decided that now is the ideal time for it, so... why not. Seattle Totems, meet Tony the Totem, your official team mascot."

Ari stood and held up the head, a stylized Thunderbird head with a large vicious beak and a tall red crest that made it look like it was aflame. She held it up next to her own head and smiled.

"Go Totems!"

Chapter Fifteen

"Is this racist?" Dale asked, staring into the wide, intimidating eyes of the mascot. She was lying on the couch, holding the head, its beak tilted down like it was about to bite into her. "I mean, at the very least it's got to be cultural appropriation, right?"

"I'm going to say yes." Ari was pacing toward the kitchen, hands in pockets, watching her feet. She wanted to make sure her performance as Tule Fletcher was convincing enough to remove any doubt. "But you could also say it supports the purpose of the totem pole. They represent myth and tell the stories of the carver's ancestors."

Dale said, "You know what else they represent? Animals that can change into another shape."

Ari looked up and smiled at her. "Then I'll be a great mascot for them even without the costume." She watched her feet. "How do I look?"

"Like you're trying too hard. You know, like in a movie when someone says to act casual and the other guy starts dancing and bopping his head because he doesn't know how to pretend to look casual? Just walk like a normal person." She sat up and put the mask aside. Put a little more of your hips into it. Good. You're leading with your shoulders. Slouch a little."

"How's this?"

"That's a lot better. I miss walking."

Ari smiled. "The doctor today said you were improving. You could be off the crutch in a few days, right?"

"Not soon enough," Dale said. "I look forward to kicking your ass jogging to work in the mornings."

"You think you can handle me? I've been training."

"I've been stockpiling my energy."

Ari sat on the couch and pushed Dale down. "Then maybe I should siphon some of it off before you're fully healed."

Dale reached up and gripped Ari's pigtails, one in each hand. "You know, with you in this get-up, it's kind of like you're a completely different person. But still Ari." She pecked Ari's lips. "That's kind of hot."

"Yeah?" Ari kissed her. "Maybe Tule Fletcher is a homewrecker."

"You know," Dale said, slipping her hands under Ari's hoodie, "a good way to figure out a character is to find out what they're like in bed."

Ari said, "Oh really?"

"I don't know. But it sounds good."

"You're damn right it does." Ari scooped Dale up, acting as a crutch for her on the way into the bedroom. She figured a little in-depth research was exactly what her character needed.

When they were catching their breath afterward, Dale teased Ari's hair. It was kinked from being in the pigtails and she brushed the ends against her lips. Ari settled with one leg across Dale's hip and kissed a spot of sweat of her shoulder. "Are you sure this is a good idea? Are you sure it's *safe*, going right into the lion's den? What if they recognize you?"

"Muldoon didn't even give a hint he might know who I am. The more I think about it, the more convinced I am that the team has no reason to know what I look like. Neither does Muldoon. All they know is a private investigator was hired to snoop around. What do they do with that information? Nothing. They pass it to Halphen, who does their dirty work for them. He's the only one who knows who I am. I'm sure Muldoon wanted to know as little as possible just so he could have deniability later."

Dale shifted underneath Ari. "What if Muldoon goes to visit him in prison? What if he describes you?"

"Deniability again. Distance. Halphen took the fall for

attempted murder. No one from the Totems organization is going anywhere near the guy."

"I hope you're right."

"Me too. But I have a pretty good sense about these things. The only person who looked even a little confused was Dubov. Even Vlcek didn't seem to notice I was the same woman he'd seen in the locker room."

Dale laced her fingers together on the back of Ari's neck. "In a couple of days, I'm going to be fully mobile. So if you need any backup, you know who to call."

"I do." She kissed Dale's cheeks and the tip of her nose. "Now that you've cheated with Tule Fletcher, how about coming home to your one true love?"

Dale dragged her bare foot up the back of Ari's calf. "Mm, I like that idea. But I've gotta say, Tule kind of makes love a lot like you do."

"Hm. Let's see if I can come up with some new moves."

"Oh, I wasn't complaining."

"Still... I'm always open to trying new things..."

Ari lingered in the parking lot until Dubov arrived. Her first day was spent watching the team practice and getting a tour of the facilities. Even though her arrival was unexpected and premature, Muldoon planned to take advantage of it. He believed the mascot was an important part of team dynamics; she needed to know the players and they needed to know her. Aulie had eventually shown up looking haggard and hungover, but he had a quick word with Muldoon and didn't get punished for his tardiness.

The entire time she was there, she'd caught Dubov casting glances her way. She knew he was eager to know her plan, but there was no way they could get a moment alone. Now they were alone in the parking lot, so she carried her costume head over to him and waited as he pulled his gear from the back of the truck. He looked at her, looked toward the rink, and kept his voice low as she fell into step beside him.

"You're pushing your luck, aren't you?"

"It's a calculated risk. I didn't want you to be alone in there."

Dubov said, "I appreciate it. For the record, no one said anything about you in the locker room. I mean..." He looked away. "I mean, they didn't say anything about you maybe being a private eye."

"So they did talk about me."

"Guys in a locker room, pretty girl wanders in. Of course they're going to talk."

Ari said, "Damn it, I tried to go for butch nerd specifically to avoid that sort of thing."

Dubov opened the door for her. "I hate to tell you this, but I think that may have helped for some of the guys."

"Men. So not worth the trouble."

"Speak for yourself."

Ari grinned at him. He had to go left for the locker rooms while she continued straight ahead into the bleachers. She had her costume in the bag again, but she couldn't change until the guys were all geared up and out on the ice. Muldoon wanted her to meet with someone, a choreographer or mascot expert or something ridiculous like that, to work out some routines. She was nervous about it. She was as coordinated as she needed to be and she knew how to skate. She had an education in skate parties stretching from fourth to seventh grade, so she was confident she wouldn't look foolish or fall on her ass. But depending on how complicated the routine was, being instructed would take focus from watching the players.

When the locker room was free, she changed into her costume for the first time. The legs were huge and the arms were thickly muscled. When she suggested the plan to Wiseman she had hoped the mascot could be female, but the costume was already made and waiting at the team owner's office, and Tony the Totem had a decidedly male physique. The arms were connected to the back by a pair of wide wings, and her feet were encased in blocky boots that were supposed to represent the bottom of the totem pole. She put her feet together, stretched her arms out to either side, and stood up as straight as possible and became a totem pole.

She was sure the image would strike fear in the hearts of every team in the NHL.

The choreographer, a woman in her fifties unexpectedly named Kimmie, arrived, and surprised Ari with the fact that very little of the practice happened on the ice. There would be halftime shows, of course, but the majority of her duties would happen in the stands. She would shoot T-shirt cannons to the crowd and interact with children. Kimmie was a former cheerleader and retired mascot for three different hockey teams. She was an expert at the art of distracting kids while their parents watched sports.

Kimmie started by telling her to run up one flight of stairs, across the aisle, and down another. Her nights as the wolf had taught her endurance so she was able to keep up with everything that was thrown at her. The costume was cumbersome and heavier than she'd expected, however, and soon she was dripping sweat.

When Kimmie took mercy and let her take a break, she sank down onto a bench to watch the players on the ice as she caught her breath. They'd split into two teams again, one side wearing orange mesh vests over their jerseys. Aulie seemed to be playing more aggressively than anyone else on the ice. Muldoon called him out on it a few times but, when it devolved into a brawl between Aulie and Max Green, the coach told Aulie to cool off in the locker room. He also benched Oborin "to keep the teams even." Ari noticed that the big Russian followed Aulie into the locker room.

Gameplay resumed. Kimmie returned to continue torturing Ari but, before she could start sprinting, something crashed to the ground in the locker room. The team were delayed by their skates and Muldoon was on the opposite side of the ice, so Ari was the closest. She hopped the partition, dropped onto a bench, and ran down the ramp. Aulie had wrapped his hands in Oborin's jersey and was in the process of swinging him against another bank of lockers when Ari arrived. Oborin hit the locker hard enough to cave in the door.

"Whoa!" Ari said. "Calm yourself down!"

"Get the hell out of here!" Aulie shoved Oborin and turned to face her. He narrowed his eyes and grunted. "Who even are you?"

She held her hands out, palms flat. "Just trying to stop an assault."

"You better watch yourself, little girl."

Aulie advanced on her. Ari braced herself for a fight she knew she would lose, given his superior size and the added benefit of the pads and gear he was wearing. She took a defensive position just before someone shoved hard past her, almost knocking her to the floor as he stepped between her and Aulie. The back of his jersey identified her savior as Vlcek, her fellow wolf. Aulie pushed back but Vlcek wouldn't be moved. He kept one hand in the center of Aulie's chest and blocked him as effectively as any football player.

"Settle down, Steve-O," Vlcek said. "Don't want to make headlines 'fore the season even starts by attacking the mascot."

"What about me?" Oborin whined, rubbing the back of his head. His accent was noticeable but not overly thick. "Guy tried to put me through a cinder block wall, for crying out loud."

Muldoon arrived at that point. He looked at Ari before examining the scene. "What the hell is going on here?"

"Someone went through my shit," Aulie said. "Took something of mine."

Oborin said, "Asshole accused me of being a thief. I didn't take shit."

Vlcek looked at Ari. She met his gaze until he looked away. By that time the rest of the team had gathered on the ramp to see what the commotion was. Ari spotted Dubov peeking around Gladstone's shoulder trying to get a view of what was happening. Muldoon also saw the crowd and turned to face them with his arms held out to either side.

"Okay, jackasses, back on the ice. You're all hockey players. You've seen fights before. Get out of here. Aulie, go wait in my office. We're going to have a talk."

Ari followed the players up the ramp. She only made it halfway before a hand gripped her shoulder hard enough that she feared it would leave a bruise. She was pulled back and slammed against the wall. Muldoon leaned close, filling her vision with his face and polluting the air between them with sour breath of tobacco and coffee.

"What were you doing in there?"

"I he-heard the fight, I was the closest..."

"You think you could've pulled those bulldogs off each other? You would've gotten your skull broke. Next time, keep your damn distance. Understand?"

Ari nodded. It was a struggle to keep her eyes wide and fearful when all she wanted to do was head-butt him. But Tule Fletcher wouldn't be that aggressive, so she had to hold back. He released her shoulder and took a step back.

"This is an internal matter for the team. You might think you're part of that, but you're really not. You're just some cutie in a costume. You're the most replaceable part of this organization."

That's what you think, Ari thought. "I understand." She forced her voice to crack. "I'm sorry i-if I overstepped my b-bounds."

"Forget it. Go, scram."

Ari hurried off the ramp and went back into the bleachers. Kimmie was watching her with wide eyes, hands on hips.

"Where did that come from?"

"What?"

"You blew off like a shot, and then jumping over the partition?" She whistled. "I was going to tell you that sometimes we have to do a little crowd control. People getting drunk and rowdy, you have to take care of 'em until security can get there. But I think we can probably skip that lesson."

Ari smiled. It was strange to be proud of doing well at a job she didn't plan to keep, but praise was praise. She reached up to massage her shoulder, ready for whatever hellish training scenario Kimmie had for her next.

At the end of the day, sore and exhausted, Ari carried the costume back to her car. The sun was almost touching the horizon and long shadows stretched across the parking lot. The security lights had flickered to life as she was going out. The players' cars were huddled near the entrance. She walked past them to where she'd parked and listened to the sound of rushed footsteps coming up from behind her. She waited until he was within arm's reach before she ducked and shifted her weight to the right. She kicked her leg out and caught Dubov on his hip.

"Oh, shit. Sorry."

"Ow! God!" He pressed a hand against his hip. "I guess I should have said 'psst' or 'the condor flies at midnight' so you would know it was me."

Ari said, "After what happened in the locker room, it would have been appreciated."

Dubov moved around to the passenger side of her car. When both doors were closed, he said, "I don't know much since they didn't really spell it out for me, but combine with what I overheard and what I know from you, Aulie's looking for the pill you took."

"I didn't know how expensive it was when I took it. I guess it was pretty obvious when one went missing. Damn."

"The bright side is no one suspects the weird new mascot chick." He chuckled. "Where'd you come up with that anyway?"

Ari shrugged. "I figured it was the only way I could get close to the team without drawing attention to myself."

"Good job on that."

She chuckled. "Yeah. Instinct, I guess."

"Anyway, I thought you'd want to know why you almost got knocked around. Coach is pissed at Aulie for being sloppy with his supply. Threatening to cut him off if he doesn't find out what happened to it. Says he threatened the whole group. I assume that meant their little drug group, not the Totems."

Ari nodded. "I've gotten everything I can from it. Maybe I could leave it somewhere so Aulie can find it so he'll stop beating up his teammates."

Dubov said, "I say keep it. If it means he can't get anything else from Muldoon, then the guys can take a few licks. Just try to stay out of their line of sight."

"I'll do that."

He opened the car door and started to lean out, then turned to look at her. "You look cute in that Totem outfit."

"Hey, watch it. My girlfriend will kick your ass if she finds out you've been flirting with me."

He smiled. "Not if Bryan beats her to the punch. Be safe, Miss... Fletcher."

"Same to you."

She watched him jog back to the rink. Stadium? Was the ice also called the arena? She would have to ask Dale again. She agreed with Dubov that it would be best to keep the pill away from Aulie, but she didn't want to risk having him go through withdrawals. Cyn could be a nasty bastard and she had a feeling Aulie would be just as nasty when he started the downward spiral. The scuffle in the locker room might just be the tip of the iceberg. She didn't want to see him at his most desperate.

CHAPTER SIXTEEN

ARI LOVED being Tony the Totem. She didn't expect that; she hadn't foreseen how much fun it would be to put on the costume and run around the bleachers, but she was having an absolute blast. She was actually disappointed that she wouldn't get to play the role with a crowd. Aulie, meanwhile, was becoming progressively more desperate to find his missing pill. He was missing practices, not that Muldoon actually let him play on the occasions he did show up. Dubov continued acting as her informant, letting her know what he overheard and what was said in the locker room.

The most important thing that happened during that stretch of days was the doctor officially took away Dale's crutch. She still needed to go easy on her left foot, but she was back to normal save for a slight limp. They celebrated by going out for a nice dinner, after which Dale proceeded to take full advantage of the fact she could once again take a dominant position in the bedroom. She might not have been fully healed, but she was definitely on the road to recovery.

The day after Dale was taken off the disabled list was the same day of the week she'd seen Muldoon and the players at Newton Ice Rink. She wanted to stake it out in case they came back so she could confirm they were using it as a drop. The only flaw in that plan was that she'd have to use another disguise, so Muldoon wouldn't recognize her or "Tule Fletcher" hanging around. Under ordinary circumstances she might have used the wolf, but she needed to be inside and take pictures if she could.

"You know... actually, no. Never mind."

"What?"

"You already have a lot on your plate pretending to be Tule. You shouldn't have to add a whole other complexity on top of it."

Ari said, "I can at least hear you out. What are you thinking?"

Dale got off the bed. She favored her right foot before she remembered her left was back in service, giving her movement an awkward sideways hop. She joined Ari at the drawer and dug around.

"This T-shirt under a baggy unbuttoned flannel. These jeans. Put on those boots you have that make you a whole foot taller--"

"An inch, at most."

Dale ignored her. "Hair in a ponytail or tucked up under the hat. You could pretend to be a guy."

Ari laughed. "I don't think I could pull that off. I know I'm not exactly buxom, but..."

"So you wear two T-shirts. Don't wear makeup."

"I don't wear enough makeup so that not wearing any will make a difference."

Dale shrugged. "Like I said, never mind. I just thought it would be a good disguise. No one would think twice about it."

"I think you just wanted to see what I'd look like as a boy."

"You'd be a sexy boy." Dale stretched out on the bed and rolled over to face her. "Just the kind of boy I like: tall and girly."

Ari laughed and swaggered over to the bed. "I'll be a boy for you."

"Mm, c'mere, boy."

Ari climbed on top of her. Dale gathered the hair that had fallen on either side of Ari's face and held it up, gathering it on the back of her head. She tilted her head to examine her features, which were shiny and scrubbed clean after her shower.

"Yeah, you're right. You're much too pretty to be a boy."

"Good thing, too. I only transform into one kind of mindless beast."

Dale laughed and used Ari's hair to pull her down into a kiss.

In the morning, Ari dressed in "grunge." She chose a baggy T-shirt, hoodie, cap, low-hanging jeans, and the boots Dale hated. She didn't shower and let her unwashed hair hang in front of her face like widow's weeds. Anywhere else in the country it would looked outdated, but hometown pride still kept Kurt's star shining brightly. The lockers were in an open area where she could see them from the lobby, so she took a seat and settled in. Whenever an employee approached her, she claimed to be waiting for a friend. She checked her phone frequently and with increasing irritation, giving her a reason to watch the parking lot for signs of Totem players or their coach.

She had been there for an hour when her phone actually rang, startling her enough that she nearly dropped it. The screen said it was Lucy Macallan, so she dropped character before answering.

"Lucy? Hey. What's going on?"

"Ariadne. Were you serious about giving me a ride if I needed one?"

"Absolutely." She scanned the parking lot again.

Lucy said, "I'm at Virginia Mason. I was supposed to get treatment today, but the numbers weren't right so they're sending me home. I made a big deal about sending Diana to work. I know she would come in a heartbeat if I asked..."

"No, it's no trouble. I can be there in fifteen minutes."

They arranged to meet at a Vietnamese restaurant near the hospital where Lucy would buy Ari lunch for her trouble. Ari cast a final look around the rink for signs of her quarry, but they remained stubbornly absent. Traffic was kind to her so, ten minutes later, she arrived outside the restaurant at the same time Lucy was coming around the corner. They both ordered the pho and took a table near the window. Lucy waited until they were seated before she asked.

"Laundry day?"

Ari smiled. "I was doing a stakeout for people who might know what I look like. They've also seen me in my usual disguise, so that wasn't an option. I had to step it up."

"I see. Teenage me probably would've been wild for you. I went through a whole Nirvana thing."

Ari said, "I never really liked their music."

"It wasn't the music. It was the string-bean with the long blonde hair playing guitar that got my interest. Of course, it didn't take me long to realize I was looking for something extra under the dirty sweater."

Ari chuckled. "I can understand that. Back when the Femme

Reapers first showed up, I had a huge crush on one of the sisters. The one who wears blue all the time."

"I can never remember," Lucy said.

"So... is everything okay? Are you...?"

Lucy nodded. "I'm fine. It's just my platelet count isn't where they wanted it to be, so I skipped the treatment today. It actually means I feel better than I would otherwise."

"Ah." Ari stirred the noodles around in her bowl. "Sorry, I'm not sure how to talk about this. I don't know if I should be consoling or--"

"Just talk to me like normal."

"I think I can do that."

Lucy said, "What are you and my wife hiding?"

Ari blinked and leaned back. "Wh-what?"

"Come on, Ariadne. I'm not stupid. And I also know neither one of you would have an affair. You love Dale too much and Diana is, like, crazy in love with me." Ari had to smile at that. "But I know there's something going on. You come by in the middle of the night and she walks to the corner just so I won't overhear anything? I know she didn't want to wake me up, but you could've just stayed on the porch if that was all she was worried about. She didn't want me walking in on the middle of whatever conversation you were having. It's not the first time she's done something like that, either. We don't keep secrets from each other."

Ari said, "It could be... a sensitive case..."

Lucy repeated, "We don't keep secrets from each other, Ariadne. When I say that, I mean she told me she thought about leaving me when I was diagnosed with cancer."

"She *what?*"

"Briefly. I was being a dark, depressing bitch and feeling sorry for myself every day. I would have wanted to leave me, too. Diana kept a brave face the whole time, but when it passed, she admitted there were moments of weakness. But she loved me too much to let one dark cloud ruin everything we've built, so we stuck in there. But the point is, if the secret was hers to tell, she would tell me. So it's your secret. I don't want Diana keeping secrets from me. If you can trust her, you can trust me."

Ari tapped her fingernail on the table. "You're right about everything. I'll just put that out there right away." Lucy nodded slowly but didn't take her eyes off Ari. "It's a hell of a secret, Lucy. And it's not something you'll believe without evidence."

"I'm willing to suspend my disbelief."

Ari handed her phone across the table.

"Call Dale. Tell her what you just told me."

"What..."

"She'll tell you my secret. Tell her I said it's okay and to just tell the truth. It's time that you knew. I should've told you when I told Diana. I'll write down what she's going to say, so you'll know we're not making it up on the spot."

Lucy looked at the phone. She sighed when she took it. "This better be a hell of a secret," she said as she dialed. Ari took out a pad and began writing where Lucy couldn't see.

"Trust me, it's a doozy."

"Hello, Dale? It's Lucy Macallan." She explained again, her eyes on Ari the entire time. "Ari told me to ask you what the secret is. She said it's time, and she should've told me when she told Diana." She listened to the low murmur of Dale's voice. A line appeared between her eyebrows.

Ari slipped her notepad across the table. She'd written, "She just told you I'm a werewolf."

Lucy read the note, looked at Ari, and then blinked. "Yes. Dale, I need to talk to your girlfriend. Thank you for telling me. I will. Goodbye." She hung up and carefully placed the phone on top of the notepad.

"I know it's hard to accept, but I promise you-"

"You're *canidae?*"

It was Ari's turn to frown. "Did Dale use that word?"

"No, she said werewolf. But if you want to be accurate..."

"*Canidae.* Right. How do you know that term?"

Lucy said, "I knew one. After college but before Diana. She was a model I used in my earliest graphic novels. She would come to my studio to pose. She could contort herself into these amazing shapes. It was perfect for me. One night she was there late, we got drunk, one thing led to another..." Her voice drifted off. "The second time we slept together, she said she had to tell me something if we were going to have an actual relationship. She told me everything about being *canidae*, about... she called it 'wolf-shifting.' I'm ashamed to admit that since she was Native American, I just assumed she was talking about some kind of ritual. Then she showed me."

She looked up at Ari, a mixture of awe and fear in her eyes.

"So. You can... you do that?"

Ari nodded. "Yeah. I can't believe you know about us. You've never told Diana? What about not keeping secrets?"

"That's... that's a lie of omission, I guess. At what point in the marriage do you bring up the fact you once fucked a werewolf?"

Ari had to laugh at that. "Good point. I'm sure Diana will understand."

"And I can't be too mad that she was keeping it secret from me." She chuckled. "We were both holding werewolf secrets. What are the odds of that?"

"This is Seattle," Ari said. "The odds are actually pretty good."

They finished their lunch and Ari drove Lucy home. Lucy thanked her again for the ride. "I'm sure it's more of an inconvenience than you're letting on. Are you in the middle of a case?"

"Actually I am, yeah. How'd you know?"

"You've got this look on your face. It's like you're wrestling with something right behind your eyes. You're trying not to let it through, but it's still seeping out."

Ari said, "You're good."

"I'm an artist. I draw faces for a living. You learn tricks."

"Well, you're wrong about one thing. It's not a case I'm conflicted by. It's a job offer. And I'm not really conflicted by it. I'm not going to take it. I've talked to everyone and I'm... I'm ninety-nine percent sure I'm not going to take it." She explained about GG&M again as they drove north.

Lucy listened. When Ari was finished, she said, "So basically it's like if someone offered me a job at one of the big comic companies. I'd still be doing what I love, and I'd be doing it for more money, but my hands would be tied in terms of content and editorial issues."

"Exactly. Everything inside me says I can't take the job. And I've decided I'm going to turn it down when the offer is made. But it's money and security. Am I being completely idiotic to turn it down for sentimental reasons? What would you do?"

"I honestly don't know." She looked out the window. "GG&M is a big firm, right? Their clients are extremely wealthy."

Ari nodded. "That's why they can afford to pay me to just sit around until they need me."

"But the people who hire you now... they can't afford GG&M. They can barely afford you, if I'm guessing right. So if you take the job at GG&M, who is going to look out for them?"

Ari was stunned into silence. "You know, Dale said the exact same thing."

"I knew I liked that lady."

"Thank you, Lucy."

When they arrived, Ari offered to stay and keep Lucy company. "Thanks, but I want to take a nap so I'll be rested when Diana gets off work. I have a feeling we're going to have a long talk tonight."

"Good luck."

She watched to make sure Lucy got into the house without trouble, then headed back to the ice rink. She hoped she hadn't missed her chance to catch Muldoon in the act, but she didn't like her odds.

Her luck was middling: Muldoon and three of the players were already there, having one of their conferences on the ice. She got close enough to see that Anton Oesterle was the one missing player. She took a seat where she could see the lockers again and took out her phone. She held it like she was typing texts, the camera's lens aimed where she could catch Oesterle when he arrived.

Ari had learned the secret to blending into a crowd was to simply be in a crowd. People were self-centered, focused on their own path, tunnel-visioned. The costume helped her avoid notice, but everything else was just settling in and looking like anyone else in the building. She planted her feet apart and slouched so she would appear to be just one of the half-dozen people milling around the public area of the skating rink.

Oesterle showed up fifteen minutes after she returned, and she whispered a small thank-you to the patron saint of private detectives and wolves. He looked hungover, carrying a duffel bag over his shoulder. As expected, he didn't even look her way as he rushed past her to the lockers. He sat on a bench, placed the duffel between his feet, and opened the locker. Ari angled her phone and opened the camera. She switched to video rather than taking still shots and filmed as Oesterle took a small white bag out of the locker and dumped it into his duffel.

It was a bittersweet moment. She had evidence confirming the theory that Muldoon was using the Newton Ice Rink as a drop-off point, but she'd missed Muldoon actually dropping it off. Still, it wasn't a complete bust. She closed the camera as Oesterle put his skates on and headed out onto the ice. He had left his duffel bag in the locker. She could risk grabbing it, but she didn't want Oesterle going over the edge like Aulie.

Her phone rang again, and she stared at it in disbelief. Maybe the rink had some kind of beacon that summoned calls. Her surprise turned to irritation when she saw who it was. She considered ignoring it, but knew the conversation had to take place eventually. She tapped the screen.

"Hello, Cecily."

"Miss Willow. I hope you're not busy."

Ari said, "Would it matter?"

"I'd like you to come in this evening so we could discuss your progress on the Totems case. I presume you are making progress, correct?"

Ari looked toward the lockers. "You could say that."

"Mr. Wiseman told me he arranged for you to be the team's mascot. It's nice to know you have an alternate career lined up just in case investigation doesn't work."

"What time do you need me there?"

"Six o'clock will be fine. Don't be late."

Ari said, "I'm counting the minutes."

"Hm."

Ari hung up on her, or vice versa, and got up to move into a position where she could see the ice. She didn't know if the information she'd gathered so far was damning enough to justify removing Muldoon and his drugged players from the team, but all she could do was provide what she'd found. She hoped for the sake of the players Muldoon had gotten hooked on a dangerous drug that it convinced the team owner to change the roster.

CHAPTER SEVENTEEN

ARI STAYED until the team left, none of them even glancing her way out of the rink. She made a note of which lockers they got their stuff from and watched as Muldoon removed a small packet from each one. She videotaped that as well. She couldn't confirm what was in the packets or what the players had taken out of the lockers, but it was at the very least shady behavior. She waited until Muldoon was gone before she left as well. She went back to the office so she could change and make dinner plans with Dale before going to GG&M.

She passed the window that looked into their waiting room and was startled to see what appeared to be a stranger sitting at Dale's desk. She stopped and realized it was Dale, but she was missing about ninety percent of her hair. The back was cut short, tapering to a V at the back of her neck. It was longer on the sides, with two narrow wings hanging down in front of her ears. Ari knocked on the glass and Dale turned to reveal she had thick bangs that covered her eyebrows. She smiled and waved.

By the time Ari made it inside, Dale was standing up and teasing her bangs. "I'm not sure about this part. It might get hung up on my glasses when I wear them."

"I think it looks great." She reached up and stroked the stubble at the nape of Dale's neck. Dale shivered pleasantly. "I thought you were only thinking about getting it cut."

"I was, but I went for a walk to celebrate the fact I can walk again..." Ari's expression changed to one of scolding. "...a short walk. It felt like the first day of summer vacation. I wanted to mark it somehow, so. I mean, hopefully you don't hate it."

Ari said, "I love it. You look beautiful." She kissed the corners of Dale's mouth. "I really like it. I mean, I'll miss the long hair and having something to hold onto from time to time. But this shows me more of your face. And your throat..." She dragged her fingers down the side of Dale's neck, making her shiver again. Ari laughed. "Sensitive?"

"Little bit, I guess."

Ari raised an eyebrow. "I'll have to take advantage of that. But later. Right now I need to get out of this get-up and put on some respectable clothes. Cecily wants me at her office at six o'clock to give her an update."

Dale followed Ari into the office. "Do you have anything new to give her?"

Ari changed while she told her about the video she'd taken. Dale took Ari's phone to the computer, transferred the footage, and took a few screenshots to print out.

Once Ari was herself again, she walked around the desk to look at the pictures as they printed out. She grimaced. "It's not exactly damning."

"It's definitely shady," Dale said.

"But it doesn't prove anything."

"Mm," Dale stood and moved out of the way. "One step closer though."

Ari nodded and took her seat. She spent the next few hours working on a progress report, listing what she'd discovered about Cyn and Muldoon's connection to it. She listed her suspicions about Halphen taking the fall to protect the flow of drugs. When it came time to list the players who were involved, she hesitated. She was all but certain who was doping and who wasn't. But were they being pressured? What if they were just representatives? Muldoon gave the drugs to four players who then passed it out to the rest of the team? In the end she decided not to name names just yet.

On her way out, she made dinner plans with Dale. Ari would drop her off at home to get ready, then come pick her up after the meeting. It would also give her time to decide where she wanted to eat, a process that took at least half an hour on a good night. She ended up in traffic and arrived at the Gilles Girard & Moreau building ten minutes after six.

The lobby was abandoned save for two women behind the front desk and a security guard posted near the elevators. She slowed as she approached him, but he nodded her on.

"Go on up. Miss Parrish said to be expecting you."

"Thanks," she said, a little surprised the guard knew her on sight. She took the elevator up and received another surprise when the doors opened to reveal Shannon was sitting at the desk. "Boss got you working overtime?"

"Something like that. Miss Parrish is waiting for you in her office."

Shannon looked like she was holding something back, but Ari didn't want to press when she was already running late. She continued through the normally-closed doors, now standing open. All of the offices she passed were dark. Not one secretary remained at any of the desks. She walked through the abandoned space to Cecily's office, the only place that was still well-lit. Ari paused at the threshold and blinked at what she saw.

Cecily was standing behind the desk facing the window. Her dress, skintight and red with black accents, was made of a material that reflected light from the setting sun. She looked like sex, like a pin-up representation of lust and desire. The woman was a succubus, Ari reminded herself, but even that didn't explain how absolutely fantastic she looked. Ari unconsciously wet her lips when Cecily turned and faced her.

"Uh," Ari said.

"You're here with the progress report," Cecily said.

Ari glanced toward Wiseman's office. "Shouldn't... uh... the guy who actually hired me... shouldn't he be here?" It was strange she couldn't think of his name, but her attention was drawn back to the strip of Cecily's right leg that was exposed by a slit in the dress.

Cecily said, "Mr. Wiseman was scolded for stepping out of bounds. He shouldn't have given you the case without discussing it with me. The case is important and there is a time element involved, which is why he's still employed with the firm, but from now on you'll be reporting to me."

"Okay."

"Sit," Cecily said. Ari moved to the seat across from Cecily's desk. Cecily remained standing, arms crossed. "Report."

Ari had an envelope with her typed report and the photos from that day at the skating rink. She handed them over and began to explain what she'd found. The more she talked, the less hold Cecily seemed to have over her. Cecily took everything out and examined it as Ari summarized. When she finished, Cecily put the pages down on her desk blotter.

"We'll have Muldoon replaced immediately. As well as the players he's supplying with this drug, once you provide those names."

"I don't think that's the right move."

Cecily brushed a stray hair away from her face as she turned her gaze back to Ari. "We're only concerned with the Totems image. We don't need to convict Mr. Muldoon. The mere implication of doping his players will be enough for Mr. Levitt to decide he isn't worth the risk. There is a list of potential replacements."

"If the owner fires Muldoon, he'll just move on to the next town and start doing this to another team. The men he's gotten addicted to Cyn here will lose their supplier. They could die."

"That's why I'm going to suggest removing them as well. Once we have their names. Your photos showed Mr. Oborin, so he's one. Who are the others?"

Ari said, "I'm not going to reveal that. And I'm not going to suggest removing Muldoon yet, either. I'm close to proving what he's been doing. We can get rid of him, make sure he never does this again, and get his players the help they need before their doping becomes fatal."

"That's not our concern. We were hired by the team to make sure they would represent the city properly. You have proven they won't. Provide the names of the people you suspect of using the drugs and they'll be replaced. At that point, your case will be closed."

Ari stood up. "I'm not going to walk away and leave these men in danger."

"I told you to sit, Miss Willow."

"Fuck you."

Cecily stepped closer. Her eyes dropped to Ari's collar and she brought her hand up to touch a finger to the leather. When she spoke again, her voice was a rumbling purr just above the level of a whisper.

"I could make you my dog."

Ari was so startled and offended she couldn't even form a

response to that.

"I could make you sit at my feet. Put you on a leash, walk you around. Would you like that?"

Ari couldn't bring herself to say no, so instead she said nothing.

"I asked you a question, puppy."

The spell was broken. Ari's hand came up and closed around Cecily's throat, just tight enough for her to know the threat was real.

"You don't get to call me that," Ari whispered.

Cecily held her gaze. Ari refused to blink first.

"You really don't want to meet my wolf, Miss Parrish."

"Very well," Cecily said. Nothing in her demeanor changed, but there was new tension in her shoulders. Ari knew she had rattled her. "You may remain on the case. Muldoon will remain with the team for the time being. Until you can find enough evidence to bring in the authorities. Is that satisfactory, Miss Willow?"

Ari dropped her hand. "Never speak like that to me again."

Cecily smoothed a hand over her hair. "I'm on my way out. Walk with me to the elevators." Ari wanted to refuse on principle, but Cecily was already walking. If she remained behind, she would be left alone in the office. She waited for Cecily to get a head start before falling into step behind her. When they got to the waiting room, Shannon was standing up behind the desk with a small plastic storage box. She glanced up as Ari and Cecily arrived and gave Ari a weak smile.

"Everything all set?" Cecily asked.

"I think so."

"Good. You are officially no longer employed by GG&M."

Ari said, "Wait, you're firing her?"

"She let you into our offices without permission. She allowed you to bribe her and promised you future unauthorized access in exchange for coffee that you were not in a position to offer. Our clients' privacy is paramount, Miss Willow, and Shannon violated that trust."

Ari said, "Look, I just didn't want to sit around for no reason. She wasn't—"

Cecily held up a hand. Her eyes hadn't left Shannon, who fitted the lid on the box with a loud click. Ari wanted to argue, but she could see there was no way for her to win.

"It's okay, Ariadne," Shannon said. "I'm sorry for violating your trust, Miss Parrish."

Cecily nodded almost imperceptibly. Shannon walked to the elevators, which arrived with blessed punctuality so she wouldn't have to stand and wait for them. Once she was gone, Cecily moved to one of the other elevators and hit the call button.

"You made her stay late just to fire her in front of me? What kind of bullshit power trip is that?"

"The same kind you played by manipulating her into letting you bypass our security. You are very much the hypocrite, Miss Willow. You storm into my office, circumventing the proper procedures, to complain that I've violated your privacy by installing security in your office. Feel free to continue playing your little games with my staff, Miss Willow. They are all replaceable."

"Message received," Ari said. "Now give Shannon her job back."

Cecily spoke without facing her. "That would defeat the purpose of my message."

Ari moved to stand in front of Cecily. "Is this because I'm not taking your job offer?"

"I wasn't aware you'd come to a final decision on that."

"Consider this your official notice."

Cecily drew in a deep breath and let it out through her nose. "That's disappointing."

"Yeah, not for me." The elevator arrived for them, but Ari brushed past her. "I think I'll take the stairs. Something tells me it would be bad for us to share an enclosed space right now."

"Good luck with your hockey team, Miss Willow. The clock is ticking."

Ari opened the door to the stairwell and departed without responding. She knew it was giving Cecily the last word, but she didn't trust herself to say anything constructive in that moment. She chose to leave the building before doing anything she would come to regret. She hurried downstairs and ran across the lobby, slowing when she passed the security guard.

"Did a woman just leave here carrying a Tupperware box?"

He pointed her in the right direction. She waved a thanks to him and ran outside. Shannon had only made it to the corner and Ari called her name. She turned and waited for Ari to catch up with her.

"I'm so sorry about that."

"It's not your fault." Shannon smirked. "Okay. It kind of was your fault. But I would do it again. That place... you follow the rules, you make Miss Parrish happy, you keep your head down and do your job. Helping you felt good. It felt fantastic to be on your side. To break the rules. It reminded me of who I was before I started working there. I'll miss the benefits, of course, but I think a new job will be a lot better for me in the long run."

Ari took out one of her cards. "Until then, sometimes I need help on stakeouts or with research. I can't pay much, but hopefully it will tide you over."

"Thanks. Honestly, they paid me so well here, I have a ton in savings. I should be fine. But I'll keep the card just in case."

Ari nodded. "Again... sorry for my part in it."

Shannon shrugged. "The only thing I'll really miss is the sex."

"The... sex?"

"With Miss Parrish." She realized Ari's confusion. "Oh. Pretty much everyone at the firm has slept with her at one point or another. I thought you figured that out when you crashed her Christmas party last year."

Ari said, "I assumed... I didn't know... *everyone* at the firm?"

"Well, not the gay men or the straight women. She just watched them have their fun."

"That's..." She furrowed her brow and wondered if it would've been a requirement of her employment as well. Given the comment about being her dog, she was fairly sure it would've been. "No, I wasn't aware of anything like that."

"Oh. It's not like she forced us."

Ari wasn't entirely sure of that. Cecily was a succubus; she could have forced anyone who was reluctant about becoming their boss' sex slave into complying. The thought made her skin crawl.

"Maybe you should be thanking me for getting you out of there."

Shannon laughed. "Maybe so. I feel like I have a clear head for the first time in... ages." She breathed in deeply and looked around at the street as if she'd just left a windowless cell. "And in the spirit of that clarity, I want to warn you. Don't work for Cecily Parrish. Not on a retainer, not on a case-by-case basis. She gets her claws in someone and she very rarely lets them go. So... I guess I do owe you for this."

"I'll keep that in mind. Good luck."

"Good luck to you. You're the one who has to go back. Take care, Ariadne."

Ari watched Shannon go, then turned and looked up. She wasn't sure which floor belonged to GG&M, but the entire glass-fronted building looked ominous in the half-light of evening. She touched her collar, only partially aware she was rubbing at the spot where Cecily had touched it.

CHAPTER EIGHTEEN

DALE CALLED, "Hey, puppy," from the bedroom as soon as Ari was through the door. She paused, grateful for the instant confirmation that Cecily hadn't ruined the pet name. Dale came out of the bedroom in a dark green blouse and a black skirt. Her hair was still a shock, but it was a very nice shock. She looked even lovelier all dolled up for their dinner. "So I have it narrowed down to two..."

Ari cupped Dale's face and kissed her hard. Dale made a surprised sound as she put her arms around Ari's waist and sagged against her. It was intended to be just a step above a hello kiss, but her anger at Cecily plus the general aura of arousal that came from spending time with the succubus combined to make her more eager. She pulled back and pulled at Dale's bottom lip with hers before flicking her tongue against it.

"How hungry are you?" Ari asked.

"Not as hungry as you are, apparently." Dale kissed Ari and moved her hands up to the middle of her back. Ari moved them until Dale's back was against the living room wall. Ari moved her hands to Dale's collar and blindly undid each button until the blouse hung open. She glanced down and saw her favorite cream-colored bra. She smiled as she brushed her fingertips over the black lace on one cup.

"Looks like you expected to get lucky tonight."

"Well, I was going to seduce you. Take the new hair out for a test drive."

"Sorry to ruin your plans."

"So far everything's going really well." She brushed her tongue across Ari's lips and pulled her in for another kiss. Ari slipped the blouse off Dale's shoulders and, as it fell, ran her fingers along the waist of her skirt in search of the zipper. Dale reached down and guided her to it and they dragged it down together. Ari stood up and dragged her fingers over the curve of Dale's hip.

"Whose am I?"

Dale was fixated on Ari's mouth but still missed the question. "What?"

Ari said, "Who do I belong to?"

"I'm..." She finally met Ari's eyes. "You're... yours?"

Ari moved her hands over Dale's ass and squeezed. She rolled her hips forward and Dale did the same, pressing herself against the smooth material of Ari's trousers. "Whose am I?"

Dale smiled. "Mine?"

"Yes." She kissed Dale and moved her away from the wall, into the bedroom.

"You're my puppy."

Ari growled and pushed Dale down onto the bed. She took off her clothes before joining her, and Dale slipped her fingers under the collar as Ari settled on top of her. Ari braced one hand above Dale's shoulder and put her other hand between Dale's legs. Dale bit her bottom lip, two fingers still curled in Ari's collar. Ari pressed two fingers against Dale's sex and pinned it there with her thigh, moving her hips slowly until Dale matched her rhythm.

"Do you want to be on top of me?" Ari asked.

"No, it's fine." Dale was breathless and her eyes drifted shut. "Don't stop."

She moaned when Ari's middle finger slipped inside of her. Ari bowed her head to kiss Dale's breasts through her bra. Dale released the collar and put her hand in Ari's hair. She wrapped it around her hand and pulled, her grunting slowly forming into the word "puppy" over and over. She came when Ari shifted two fingers to tease her clit. Ari watched the way her face changed, the wrinkle between her eyes and the pink that rose from her collar up into her cheeks. Her lips pulled back and she pushed her head down into the pillow.

They were both still breathing hard when Dale shifted positions. She lifted her hips and settled on Ari's thigh before she pulled Ari down on top of her. Ari kissed her and Dale began to move her lower body with her leg trapped between Ari's.

"Whose am I?" Dale asked.

"Mine," Ari whispered against her mouth.

"Thank you, puppy," Dale whispered back. "Now come for me. Please."

Ari moved her lips to Dale's neck and sought out a particularly sensitive spot, brushing away the sweat with her tongue before she began sucking on it. Dale cried out helplessly against the assault and dug her fingers into the tight muscles of Ari's flank, above her hips but below her ribs. It was difficult to tell who was riding whom, but Ari's spine curved and lengthened in a serpentine stretch when she came. She closed her eyes and trembled as she felt the orgasm wash over her. Her arms were weak and her face was tingling.

She collapsed on top of Dale and panted heavily, aware only when she lifted her head of what had happened. Dale was laughing, one hand on top of Ari's head and the other ruffling the fur on her back.

"Well," Dale whispered against Ari's furry snout. "*That* has never happened before."

Ari concentrated and felt her bones popping back into place, shifting from canine to bipedal. The pain was worse than usual, but that was the price she paid for two concurrent transformations in such a short window. Once she was capable of speech she smiled and sheepishly kissed Dale's lips.

"I guess you just made me lose control. The wolf thought I was letting it out to play."

"Mm, kinky," Dale said. "I did like having all that fur on my skin. It was like getting covered up with a nice warm blanket."

Ari rolled to the side and ruffled Dale's hair as she settled on the mattress next to her. Dale put her hand on Ari's stomach and moved it in slow circles.

"What was all that 'mine' stuff? Not that I object, it's just not normal for us."

"Cecily Parrish. She went on this bizarre power trip. She said she could make me her dog." She grimaced just remembering it.

Dale said, "Gross."

"Worse than that is that she called me puppy. I was afraid she'd ruined it, but then I walked in and you immediately took it back. Made it yours again." She brushed her thumb over Dale's cheek. "Thank you for that, sweetheart."

"Sure."

"Roll over." Dale did as she was told and Ari spooned her. She kissed the newly-short hair at the back of Dale's head. She moved one hand down between Dale's legs, covering her mound, and the other up to her breast. Dale squirmed and reached back to rest her hand on Ari's hip.

"Again?"

"If you want me to."

Dale said, "Kiss my neck."

"But I love your hair."

"Please, puppy."

Ari smiled and changed her angle of assault. Dale covered Ari's hand with hers and guided her fingers until she stiffened, turning her head to stifle her moans in the pillow.

"You can be loud," Ari whispered.

"Neka's upstairs."

"Let her listen."

Dale chuckled breathlessly. "Maybe another night." She pulled away from Ari so she could flip around. They embraced and began to kiss lightly, catching their breath and letting the sweat dry on their skin. Dale nuzzled Ari's cheek and settled against her. "I'll have to shower again if you still want to go out. We have some Bistro leftovers in the fridge. Portuguese chicken?"

Ari said, "Oh, I could eat some chicken."

Dale pinched Ari's hip and sat up. She put on a T-shirt and her underwear. Ari dug a pair of shorts out of the drawer and pulled them on, electing to go topless into the kitchen. Dale was used to her casual nudity, a side effect of her *canidae* upbringing, and said nothing when she came wandering in mostly-nude. They warmed up the chicken and took it to the dining room table they so rarely got to use. Ari sat, planted her feet in the seat, and let her knees stick out to either side like she was a gargoyle perched on the side of a building. Dale was a bit more proper and crossed one leg over the other.

"You know, there was more to that whole... 'mine-yours' thing. Over lunch, Lucy and I talked about her relationship with Diana. She called Diana her wife. She was Diana's wife, Diana was her wife. And then she called you my girlfriend."

Dale chewed slowly and watched her.

"I know we've discussed marriage, we've both agreed it's not something we needed. But. Girlfriend. It just sounded so unofficial. Temporary. We live together, we work together. You're so much a part of my life that I can't imagine it without you. My opinion on marriage hasn't changed. I don't think we need a piece of paper or a big church ceremony or whatever. But I want something to prove how committed I am to you. Even if it's just you and me there."

Dale smiled. "I would really like that, Ariadne. Like a hand-fasting, maybe?"

"I don't know. Something. We can work out the details later. I just wanted to run it by you, see how you felt about it."

"I feel... I feel like it's unnecessary, because I know how much I love you even when you're frustrating or we're angry with each other. I know there's nothing that would change that. I know what we have is different from anything I've ever felt before. I know you're not just my girlfriend, too. So yeah. Whatever you decide to do, I'll stand up with you."

Ari reached over for Dale's hand. She was wearing her bracelet made of intertwined strands of Ari's hair and the wolf's fur.

"So will I have to change my name?"

"Only if you want to. Dale Willow?"

"Ari and Dale Will-fry."

Ari laughed. "Frillow."

"Frillow. Sounds badass."

Dale smiled. "I think we'll stick with our own names for now."

"Sure."

"So what are you going to do about the Totems?"

Ari grunted and shook her head. "I'm going back to the skating rink tomorrow. Hopefully I can talk someone into giving me access to their security cameras."

Dale said, "They have cameras pointed at the lockers?"

"Sure. People are just changing their shoes, locking up their valuables so they won't fall out onto the ice. Stuff like that. No one's actually changing clothes. Weren't you wondering how I was able to watch them put stuff in and take it out?"

Dale shrugged. "I just assumed you'd perfected that 'dude' disguise I keep asking you to try."

Ari smiled. "You're not going to let that go, are you?"

"You'd be the sexiest dude ever."

"I think you just want to butch me up."

"Mm-hmm."

Ari laughed and flicked a piece of rice across the table.

The next morning, she drove to Newton Ice Rink as soon as it opened. She wanted to try getting the security footage before she had to spend another day rehearsing to be Tony the Totem. The main doors were already unlocked when she arrived, but no one had shown up yet to start skating. She recognized the curly-haired kid behind the counter from her first visit and she struggled to remember his name. She had already recalled it by the time she was close enough to read his nametag.

"Patrick, right?"

"Yes." He stared for a moment before recognition dawned. "Oh, you were here a week or so back. You were scoping the place out for a birthday party or something. Did you want to leave a deposit?"

"Not exactly. I'm afraid I kind of lied to you. I'm actually a private investigator."

Patrick's eyes widened. "In real life?"

"Yeah, in real life. I think someone's been using your facility to conduct criminal business. I've been trying to catch them in the act, but so far I haven't had any luck. I just can't manage to be here at the right time. So here's what I'm hoping you can do for me. I want to take a look at your security tapes. I can do it here so you don't need to give me possession of them. I just need to confirm it's happening in order to take the next step with my investigation."

"I don't know." He looked helplessly toward the manager's office. "We're supposed to ask for a warrant or, like, an official police presence."

Ari said, "I could do that. But then it would go in my report, the news might get wind of it, and then this place becomes known as that skating rink where those criminals hang out."

The odds of anything like that happening were tiny, but she could see it had gotten through to him. He drummed his fingers on the table and then gestured for her to come around the counter.

"If anyone asks, this never happened. What do you need to look at?"

She told him the dates. "Everything we're about to do is off the record, confidential. I can't let these guys know I'm looking at them, okay?"

"Sure, you can count on me."

He led her to a desk made of printed laminate designed to look like wood. There was an old PC sitting on one corner and she grimaced in anticipation of the video's quality. Patrick put the keyboard on his lap and poised his fingers over it before he started typing. He accessed the security records.

"Okay, those dates again? Times of day?"

She told him and he opened a folder. Rows of thumbnails lined up across the screen. "Oh, wait. These are the days Mr. Muldoon and his friends are here." He looked at her. "Is Mr. Muldoon the guy you're looking at?"

"Remember your promise to keep this confidential?"

Patrick looked at the screen again. "Sheesh. I wouldn't have expected that. Okay, so if you're looking for him, I have a pretty good idea of where to look. He keeps a regular-ish schedule." He typed again and opened one of the thumbnails. He scrolled forward until he saw something he recognized, went back, and hit play. Ari watched as a group of people milled about in the lobby. Finally, a man in a windbreaker and a baseball cap approached the counter.

Patrick pointed. "That's him. He always wears that windbreaker."

"Tell me he doesn't wear that cap the entire time he's here."

"Uh..."

They followed him to the locker area. He stopped at four and repeated the same procedure at every one: twist the combination lock, open the door, place a small packet inside, then replace the lock.

"He's here for about an hour, hour and a half every time. Depends on when his boys show up." They watched as Oborin and Aulie showed up and retrieved the packets from the lockers while leaving packets of their own. They geared up and went out onto the ice. As Patrick predicted, fifty-five minutes later, the team left. Muldoon went back to the lockers and opened them again to retrieve what had been left behind.

"Oh, shit," Patrick said. "That's a definite drop. Shit!"

Ari was too busy watching what Muldoon did next. After emptying the lockers, he sat on one of the benches and took an iPad out of his bag. He unlocked it and began tapping the screen.

"He kept a record." She remembered seeing him with the iPad at the Tukwila rink. He kept it in a bag near the bench. If he kept track of every pickup and drop-off, she could end the case right then and there. She could name every player who had ever bought Cyn while taking Muldoon down as their dealer. "Listen, Patrick, can you take screen shots with this?"

"Sure."

She gave him her card. "Get as many pictures as you can of Muldoon and anyone who takes the packages out of the lockers he leaves something in. Email them to the address on the card."

"Okay. Hey, are these guys dangerous?"

Ari started to shake her head, but she remembered Aulie freaking out in the locker room. "I don't think they'll do anything to hurt you. They don't have any reason to if they don't know about you helping with the tapes. So just keep quiet."

"Will do."

Ari thanked him and left the rink. She would be late for mascot practice, but hopefully it was going to be her final day. Her goal now was to get her hands on Muldoon's iPad so she could nail him to the wall with it. The pictures from Patrick would be a good backup plan or icing on the cake when she took her evidence to GG&M. Once he was out and the players were safe, she could cut ties with the law firm and everything could get back to normal.

CHAPTER NINETEEN

KIMMIE WAS pissed at her for being late, but Ari apologized profusely. The team was already on the ice, running drills from the looks of it. Ari practiced as well but she couldn't keep her mind on what she was doing. Eventually Kimmie took pity on her and suggested a twenty-minute break. They sat together in the section behind one of the goals and watched the team. Kimmie had a couple of energy drinks and offered one to Ari.

"Sorry about this," Ari said. "I guess my head just isn't in the game."

"Don't worry too much about it," Kimmie said. "If you have to force it, you should probably take a step back. Advice for practice, working out, friendships, whatever."

"It's good advice." She took a sip of her drink. Aulie had apparently gotten off Muldoon's shit list because he was suited up and playing with the others. "Can I ask you something, hypothetically?"

Kimmie nodded.

"How do you feel about performance enhancing drugs?"

"You touch anything like that, I'll fucking kick your ass out of the building myself." Her voice was suddenly clipped, like stones clacking together. She twisted to look at Ari. "Are you doing anything right now? Is this a crash?"

Ari held up her hands. "No. No, it really was a hypothetical. I just wanted to know how you felt about it. I think I get the picture."

"I'm going to recommend drug testing because of this conversation. Just to cover my bases. I've seen mascots and athletes both abuse that shit. It's like taking a pill that lets you fly, but only straight up, and you can only keep in the air if you keep taking it. Eventually you're going to run out. The higher you are when that happens, the harder you're going to hit the ground."

Ari looked out at the ice. Muldoon's bag was on the bench, unprotected. He and the team were on the opposite side of the rink.

"I need to level with you, Kimmie. I'm not a mascot."

"Not yet, anyway. With a little more practice~"

Ari said, "I meant I'm here for another reason. You remember Aulie going ape-shit in the locker rooms? It's because one of his pills went missing."

Kimmie looked at her long and hard before she responded. "And?"

"I took it. I needed someone to tell me what it was. Now I need proof that Muldoon is the one who gave it to him."

"Muldoon?"

Ari put a hand on Kimmie's arm. She could feel the muscles tensing in anticipation of rising up and jumping own onto the ice.

"Hold on. There's no reason to go running off half-cocked. There's evidence. We can take him down for good, nice and legally. All I have to do is get into his duffel bag. There's an iPad in there with a list. Who bought how much of it and when. I can use that to bring him down and get the players who are using the help they need to get off of it."

Kimmie chewed her bottom lip and narrowed her eyes. "I can distract him if that's what you need."

"If anything goes wrong, you run like hell. I don't want them taking it out on you if they catch me snooping."

She didn't look happy, but she nodded. They stood up together and Kimmie went left, Ari went right. Muldoon and the rest of the team had long since learned to ignore their antics in the bleachers. Ari felt practically invisible, but she was grateful to have someone running interference just in case. She kept her gait casual, grateful she was still in street clothes and not the ridiculous mascot costume. When she got to the players' bench, she slipped over the barrier and stepped down, immediately dropping into a crouch to approach

Muldoon's bag.

Ari looked to make sure Kimmie was in position before she began searching. She was on the opposite side of the rink and, when she saw Ari, she unzipped her track jacket and shrugged it off her shoulders. She was wearing a sports bra underneath and, despite being middle-aged, her body was worthy of distraction. A few players glanced over, nudged the player next to them, and soon as least half the heads on the ice were turned toward the woman who seemed to be innocently doing her stretches.

Ari opened the bag and reached inside. The iPad was sitting right on top of everything, protected by a red leather cover. She closed her fingers around it and started to pull.

"Hey, what the hell is she doing?"

Ari thought she recognized Noel Harden's voice, but didn't waste time by looking over to confirm. She pulled the iPad free, stood up, and ran for the locker room. She heard the swish of skates on ice and the clatter of sticks being thrown down. She had a mental map of the building and planned her route as she ran down the ramp. Through the locker room, out into the service corridor, through the big double doors to the main lobby, then outside. Then, if she could block the doors or otherwise slow their pursuit, she would go to the car. If not, she would run alongside the building into the woods. If she couldn't shake them, the wolf sure as hell could.

Her plan began to fall apart once she got past the locker rooms. The double doors to the main lobby were locked, so she had to keep running. The team's shouted voices echoed off the cinder block walls of the locker room, but she couldn't make out what they were saying. She heard gear being thrown to the side as it was shed and tossed aside. She revised her escape route; there was a door leading out to the parking lot she could use.

A door opened in front of her and Oborin stepped out. Ari slammed into him, unable to stop, and spun to the side. He was so startled that he backed up into the door and closed his arms around the empty space she had just vacated. She kept a death grip on the computer, holding it to her chest like a quarterback going for the game-winning goal. Oborin shouted to his friends that he was "right on top of her," and his voice really did sound like it was right in her ear.

"Stop that bitch!" Muldoon shouted. The echo was so bad that she couldn't tell if he was ahead of her or behind.

She didn't feel the hand in her hair until it was pulled taut. She cried out as her forward momentum was suddenly stopped, but she spun around and faced Oborin. She brought the iPad up and drove the sharp edge of its side into his forehead. He cried out and let her go, stumbling back with both hands over the strip of blood that was welling up where she'd hit him. She turned and saw a door that miraculously opened when she put weight against the press-bar.

Now in the lobby, she had a clear route to freedom. Hoping and praying she hadn't damaged the computer against Oborin's skull, she found reserves of energy and put on an extra burst of speed.

She was halfway to the exit when something slammed into her hard enough that she momentarily wondered if she had somehow been hit by a truck. She was knocked off her feet and landed hard, rolled head over ass, and then skidded a few feet across the linoleum like the world's largest puck. She had lost her grip on the iPad but the pain in her back and shoulder was too distracting for her to care at the moment. Heavy footsteps pounded into the lobby and she could tell she was surrounded.

"Up," Muldoon said. "Get her up. Get her on her fucking feet."

Someone grabbed her under the arms and hauled her up. As soon as she was standing, someone else punched her. She'd been punched before, but the power and anger behind the blow was literally staggering. Ari's knees immediately unlocked, her entire body sagged in the direction of her punch, and whoever was holding her up almost went down with her. Her bells were still ringing when he punched her again. This time she felt the wet tickle of blood at her nose and across her bottom lip. She went limp and let her puppeteer support her weight.

"No, Steve, twice was enough," Muldoon said.

"Steve," Ari said. "Steve Aulie. That's the one who punched me? Okay. I'll keep that in mind. Remember that, Steve-o, that'll come up later."

Aulie said, "Shut the fuck up, thief."

Ari turned her head and spit blood at him. Her hair was in her face and her vision was alarmingly blurry. She hoped the punch hadn't knocked anything loose, but at the moment she had more pressing concerns. The entire team had gathered in the lobby. Most of them looked confused, but there were enough angry faces for her to be legitimately afraid. She flipped her head to get the hair out of her face, alarmed by how much that simple gesture hurt, and scanned the men until she found Muldoon.

"Oh, was that your bag? My bad."

Muldoon didn't take his eyes off her. "Oesterle, take her into the main office. Lindholm, Aulie, help him out. And someone find Oborin. Everybody else, back on the ice."

Oesterle, the man who was apparently holding her up, hauled her forward. The whole Newton Five, an empty office, and her with no backup. The odds were bad enough that she couldn't even think of a quip to put her mind at ease as they dragged her out of the lobby.

The office was unfinished and unfurnished, with only a metal folding chair and a makeshift desk made of plywood sitting on buckets occupying the space. Oesterle dumped her in the chair and moved behind her. He crossed her wrists and was able to hold them together with one hand.

"Give me something to tie her up with."

Lindholm said, "Sorry, I left my handcuffs in my other uniform."

"Shut the hell up and give me a shoelace or something."

Ari's head had cleared somewhat, but the pain was beginning to radiate through her. "You guys really aren't thinking this hostage situation through. I'll be sure to mention that on Yelp."

"Shut the hell up," Oesterle said again.

"Kind of a broken record."

Aulie came into the room, eyes locked on her as he closed the door. He had a skate dangling from one hand. "Who are you really? You're not the mascot. You come here to snoop on us?" He bent down, lining up their faces. "You the one who stole my pill? Huh?"

Ari returned his gaze without saying anything. Oesterle was still holding her hands.

"Thieves like you need to be taught a lesson. Old school. You know how sharp our skates are?" He lifted the skate so she could see the edge. Ari instinctively leaned away from it. "I knew a guy in San Jose, fell down during a game. One of his teammates accidentally skated over his hand." He winced and made a "fllp" noise with his lips. "All four of his fingers, sliced right off. They managed to sew them back on, but they never looked the same. Like little fat sausages."

Oesterle said, "Jesus, Steve."

Aulie glared over Ari's head at him. "This little bitch almost got away with Coach's computer. You know what's on that, right? You know what she could've done with that?"

Muldoon came into the office, also glaring at her. Oborin was right behind him, holding a bloody towel to his forehead.

"So who are you?" Muldoon asked. "Journalist? Groupie? How'd you convince Ike to hire you, because you're sure as hell no mascot."

Ari said, "Consider me karma."

Muldoon gestured to Lindholm. "Go check her car. See if you can find out who she is."

Lindholm left. Once he was gone, Aulie put down the skate and reached for her pockets. She squirmed away from him. "Hey, watch it, handsy."

"Don't flatter yourself," he said as he pulled out her wallet and phone. He flipped through the wallet, but her identification was outside in the car. When he tried to unlock the phone, he was prompted to enter the password. "What's the code?"

Ari said, "U-Y-K-U-C-O-F. Have fun unscrambling it."

He took a step forward, but Muldoon stopped him. "You're the only one who has broken any laws here, Miss 'Fletcher.' You stole from me. The boys here are just being overzealous in defending my property. I appreciate that. Thank you, boys. But there's no reason to make this antagonistic. Just tell us who you are and why you wanted my iPad. Maybe we can still have a good laugh at this and let you go. No harm, no foul."

"You saw your boy tackle me out there, right?"

"Like I said. Overzealous. Do you want to sue him for injuries you received while stealing from us? I'm not sure that would go over well for you."

Lindholm came back in. "Olsson had already gotten into her car. Broke her window though." He smirked as he handed over a card. "Bitches Investigation."

Aulie snorted. "Appropriate name, at least."

Muldoon read the card and then flipped it at her face. All pretense was gone now. "You're that fucking private eye who's been looking into the team. I thought Halphen scared you off."

Aulie twisted to look at the coach. "Wait, there was a private eye investigating us? When were you going to tell us that?"

"I thought it was taken care of."

Oesterle said, "This bitch showing up out of nowhere wasn't suspicious?"

"Halphen dealt with everything. I just assumed it was a guy, not a ninety-pound cheerleader."

Aulie looked at her again. "So you *were* the one who stole my pill."

"Ariadne Willow, private investigator. And yeah, I know all about how you're doping the team with Cynosylline. Do they know about all the bodies you've left in your wake? Detroit and Phoenix. Those are the ones we know about. How many more are there, Muldoon?"

"This..." He sighed and shook his head. "This isn't how I wanted things to go. Who else knows about the Cyn?"

"Enough to guarantee you'll never coach again."

He held up a finger. "One more chance, Miss Willow. Who else knows what you've found out?"

"You'll understand if I keep that to myself."

"Okay. Steve."

She didn't see the blow coming. Aulie was already swinging when he twisted back around. His fist connected with her jaw. Oesterle tightened his grip to keep her from falling out of the seat, but her brain clicked off before he finished the follow-through.

Dale texted Ari with 'Lunch?' around noon. She assumed Ari was still in Tukwila, but she liked making the offer just in case. She waited half an hour before she warmed up some leftovers and at it at her desk. She had just finished when an email arrived in the official Bitches account. Someone named HatTrick@NewtonIce had sent them an email with the subject line Re: Security. "Ariadne, here are the pictures I was able to get. Some of them are blurry but I couldn't enhance. Is that real BTW? Zoom and enhance? Anyway I hope these work for you. If not there are more." Dale clicked through them and downloaded the best of the bunch. Muldoon and four Totem players involved in an exchange at the rink's locker area.

She went into Ari's office to use the high-quality printer, running off three copies of each picture on photo-quality paper. One copy would go in their files, one to GG&M, and the other would go to the authorities. Once they were all collated and labeled properly, she went back to her desk. She distracted herself with work and only looked at the clock once, maybe twice an hour until it started getting closer to four. She told herself Ari had gotten caught up at the rink and locked up the office.

She was still enjoying the sensation of walking without the aid of a crutch, but she still called an Uber to take her home. She watched TV for an hour before she texted Ari again. 'Update?' She waited another half hour before she started making dinner. While it cooked she called Ari and listened to the line buzz in her ear. She transferred the food she cooked to Tupperware and put it away without eating any of it. She called Ari again. She texted. Mostly she paced and chewed her fingernail. The pain in her ankle returned, but she thought it was probably just in her head.

Finally, she took out her phone and called Diana. "Hi, Dale. Everything all right?"

"I... don't know. I'm not sure." She explained the situation, along with the fact that Ari had been silent all day. "When she's working she can go a few hours without responding to a text, especially if she's working undercover. But it's night, it's dinner time, and not even a text from her saying she's going to be late. I know you have your own stuff going on~"

"Where are you? Are you at home?"

Dale wiped at her eyes before any tears could fall. "Yeah."

"Stay put. I'll be there as soon as I can."

"Lucy..."

"Lucy is fine. I'm out the door right now."

Dale sniffled. "Thank you, Diana."

She went outside and waited in the driveway. When Diana arrived, she got in the passenger seat and told her where Ari had been going the last time they spoke. They got onto I-5 and fell into silence. Dale didn't want reassurances that Ari was okay; she knew it would just be hollow comfort and she was grateful Diana wasn't offering it. But after a few minutes, the silence became oppressive.

"So... h-how is, uh, how is Lucy handling the whole wolf reveal?"

"I was more surprised than she was, actually. She's known about wolves longer than I have. It's like being the last kid on the block to find out about Santa Claus." She shifted in her seat. "It feels really good to finally have it out, though. I didn't even realize how much it was weighing on me until the weight lifted."

Dale nodded and looked out the window. "Ari and I have been talking about doing something like you and Lucy did. Maybe not marriage, but... something. Some kind of ceremony."

Diana said, "Well, you two are the most married couple I know. Might as well make it official."

When they reached the Tukwila exit, Dale took out her phone

to look up where the rink was located. She gave Diana directions and soon they had pulled into the parking lot. Dale's chest tightened when she saw there was only one car present, parked under a security light as if it was a prop left onstage after a play ended. Diana pulled up behind it and they both got out. The driver's side window was broken.

"Wait, don't..."

Dale looked at her. "Don't... touch anything? In case it's a crime scene?"

"It definitely is a crime scene," Diana said. "Someone broke into the car. We don't know what that means yet. We don't know that it means anything. Tukwila has a pretty high crime rate for a town of this size. Let me just... I'll call it in."

Dale stayed back and looked at the car, trying to see into the past. When that didn't work, she turned and looked at the dark and abandoned rink. She'd last heard from Ari seven hours earlier. At some point during the day, something had obviously gone horribly wrong. Ari had gotten into tight spots before, and she always managed to get out of it. She was captured by Wayne Corbett, she was imprisoned by assholes who dosed her with wolfsbane, and she'd escaped both times.

But Ari had only gotten out of those situations because Dale found her, Dale went looking and saved her at the last moment. She'd already been gone for hours and Dale had no idea where to even start looking. Behind her, she could hear Diana on the phone with Tukwila Police.

"~ctive Diana Macallan with the Seattle PD. I think we have a missing person in your city..."

CHAPTER TWENTY

SHE'D WOKEN up briefly in the car, but whoever was sitting beside her pushed a pill into her mouth and then squirted a water bottle between her lips. She swallowed rather than drown and soon slumped over again. When she regained consciousness a second time, the world seemed to be unsettled. Her body seemed to be swaying even though she was lying still. It hurt too much to open her eyes, but she knew her arms were handcuffed above her head in a stress position. Her muscles throbbed but didn't hurt, which worried her. She could hear the players talking on the other side of a thin wall.

The first voice was Lindholm. "~fuck girls when they're like that? Why not just break into the damn morgue? At least then you have less chance of getting caught."

Oborin said, "Hello? DNA?"

"Fuck, man, there will be DNA even if you rape her."

"Whatever. We're just lucky I had the pills or else Anton would've had to keep knocking her out. Coach wouldn't have liked that very much."

Ari's head rolled forward. She couldn't get her bearings. The room felt like it was on a caster, constantly spinning around her as a central point. Her skull was throbbing. Everything hurt, but especially her shoulders and her ass. She shifted her weight and finally opened her eyes. She was in an oak-paneled room with a leather couch along one wall. The windows were oddly shaped, like car windshields. But she wasn't in a car; she was in a room. She was seated with her back against a bar. The counter extended overhead, and the metal base of two stools framed her line of sight like bars on a jail cell. The part of the sky she could see through the window was purple-gold with dusk, but she could see no buildings to identify where she was. The smell of salt water was incredibly strong.

Oesterle was sitting across from her. He noticed her movement and stood up, moving toward the door. "Hey. She's awake."

Muldoon shouldered his way into the room. Behind him, she could see Aulie glaring at her before the door was closed on him. Muldoon walked forward and crouched in front of her.

"Welcome back, sunshine. How's your head?"

Ari blinked slowly. "So what's the game here? You gonna kill me? Cover up drug use with murder? All your boys agree with that plan?"

"They'll do what I say. Because what I say protects them, keeps them safe."

"How well did that work out for the guys you left behind in Arizona and... a-and the other one. Detroit state." She squeezed her eyes shut. The world continued to sway and roll. She raised her voice. "Did you guys do your research on the pills he's shoving down your throats? You know what it does when you stop taking it? When Muldoon moves to the next city and you're stuck paying for your own supply? And when the cash runs out, well... well, he's a ghost by then, so what does he care?"

Muldoon said, "Who have you told about this? Who knows about the pills? Who hired you?"

Ari said, "Gonna kill all of them? That's a lot of murders. You guys want to take turns, or has one of you always wanted to be a serial killer?"

"I looked up your agency while you were out. I like that cute little redhead you work with, Dale Frye. You share a home address, too. I bet she knows everything about your business. Or if not, there was a little pillow talk going on. Either way, we'll pay her a visit once we take care of you. Tell us who else knows and we'll make sure whatever happens, it's painless. Quick. Maybe we'll just pay them to keep quiet. Everyone gets to live. But if we have to work for it, the boys might want a little something extra for their efforts. Oborin has plenty of pills to go around."

Ari's focus tightened as soon as he said Dale's name. The more he spoke, the more her blood pounded in her skull. She focused on him despite the fact the floor still seemed unsteady.

She forced her eyes to lock onto him despite the swimming in her skull. "You'll die bloody."

He patted her cheek and smiled. "We've got time." He pushed himself up and walked back to the door. "We'll want to wait until full dark before we do anything. Everyone's got a camera now, even way the hell out here. Anton, keep an eye on her."

"Out here?" Ari said. "Where exactly is that?"

"That doesn't concern you." He opened the door and Ari looked past him to see a white, waist-high wall topped with a wooden rail. Panic seized her as she recognized it as the railing on Lindholm's boat. Her head wasn't unsteady; the world really was swaying from side to side. She was on a boat. They were taking her out into Georgia Strait or the ocean but it didn't matter. They were going to put her in the water.

Panic overtook her. She pulled on the chain holding her hands over her head. "Wait. Stop, that's... don't do this. Please."

Muldoon ignored her and pulled the door shut behind him. Before it closed she saw someone move along the railing. It was a brief glimpse but it was enough for her to recognize Dubov, the one player she thought she could count on as an ally. She dropped her head and tried not to despair. If they were out on the water, if she was surrounded by people who were willing to kill in order to keep their secret, then she really didn't see a way out. No one knew where she was. Hell, she didn't even know where she was. There was no rescue coming.

"This is going to hurt," she whispered.

Oesterle moved off his seat and took the position Muldoon had taken in front of her. "Don't say that, sweetie. It'll all be fine. We'll chuck you off the boat so Phil doesn't have any blood to clean up, then Coach will just shoot you in the head once you're in the water. Nice and quick. If you cooperate, tell us who else you told about our pills, we can give you another one of Kris' roofies before you go over. You'll sleep through the whole thing."

Ari shook her head. "I didn't mean that. I just... my arms are killing me right now. I think what I'm about to do is going to hurt like a motherfucker, but I don't see any other option."

He glanced at the cuffs and shifted his weight. "What you're going to do? What~"

Ari closed her eyes and shifted her arms. She screamed as the anguished nerves were shocked into an unexpected shift, her human muscles pulling and twisting until her arms were narrower and her hands had become paws. She pulled them free of the cuffs and, eyes tearing up, forced an instant shift back to human hands. Pain shot from the center of every finger and radiated through her palms and up her arms in waves of electricity.

Oesterle's eyes widened and he fell backward, but Ari was faster. She grabbed his shirt collar with one hand, clapped the other over his mouth, and threw herself against him. They fell to the ground with her on top. She brought her legs up to the soft fleshy part of his torso between his ribs and hips and squeezed. He pelted her side with punches and tried to buck her off, but she held on tight. Muldoon's threats echoed in her head. What he would do to her, what he would do to Dale and Diana. She bared her teeth and squeezed tighter, watching his eyes slowly go flat as she cut off his air. They were going to dump her in the water. Adrenaline surged through her at the thought, rage overriding fear as Oesterle's eyes finally rolled back in his head and his body went limp.

She stood up but kept her head down so no one could see her through the windows as she moved to the door. Her arms hung like baseball bats that had been nailed to her shoulders. She flexed her fingers in an attempt to get feeling back into them. Muldoon was onboard, along with Oborin and Lindholm. She'd seen Dubov, a fact which broke her heart, and she had to assume Aulie came along for the ride.

If she ran out onto the deck she would be swarmed in seconds. She couldn't take down five hockey players by herself, especially in her current condition. She debated transforming into the wolf, but decided it wouldn't be worth the risk. There were too many variables to account for. If any of them had a gun, if there were more men than she knew about, she needed to keep her head clear to make split-second decisions. Her life might depend on it.

There wasn't much in the way of weaponry in the room where they'd put her. It made sense; no one was going to put their prisoner in the armory. But there was nothing, a blunt object or something heavy she could use to her advantage, she could see to make use of. She worried it was the head trauma and drugs she'd been given affecting her brain. If she had a concussion... she couldn't think about that. She took a deep breath and scanned her options again. An empty table, a coffee urn that looked like it would cave in if she tried to hit someone with it, a tarp, some cleaning supplies.

She was debating whether she could spray some of the cleaner in their eyes when the door swung open. She had been crouching on the hinge-side, so she was out of sight when Oborin stepped into the room. "The fuck..." She saw his weight shift as he turned to look behind the door and her plan suddenly became very simple. It didn't matter how big her opponent was; he was still being supported by two very fragile ankles. She braced her arms against the wall and, just before he turned, shot her leg out straight and kicked his ankle with all the strength she could muster. She heard something pop and Oborin shouted as he went down.

Ari hurled herself at him like a pinball. She wrapped her arms around his head and dropped, pulled him down to the floor, and bounced his head off the ground. Oborin had one arm free and wrapped it around her. His other hand came up into her hair and yanked her head back. He growled as he hurled her away from him. New pain bloomed through her body as she hit the ground. She looked up as Oborin struggled to get off the floor only to fall back down when he put weight on his ankle.

Her victory was short-lived when Aulie appeared in the doorway. He looked at his fallen teammates and then spotted Ari. Dubov came into the room behind Aulie.

Aulie said, "Goddamn it, Anton, you had one job!"

Ari doubted she could take one of them, let alone both at once, but she'd go down fighting. She pushed herself up on shaky arms just in time to see Dubov wrap an arm around Aulie's neck. Aulie coughed and flapped his hands against his teammate's beefy forearm but Dubov effortlessly put Aulie into a full nelson. He squeezed until Aulie was on his knees. He only let go when Aulie dropped both arms and went limp.

Dubov looked at her and held out his hands. He spoke in a rushed whisper. "I'm on your side. I swear. I saw everything that was happening back at the arena. I knew these idiots were going to do something, so I told them you had dirt on me, too. I mean, it's technically true. I just wanted someone here to have your back if things went sour."

Ari said, "When was that going to be, Tyler? When they roofied me? When they beat the shit out of me in the coach's office?" He averted his gaze. "Forget it. We have bigger problems. Who else is onboard?"

"Just Muldoon and Lindholm. They're at the other side of the boat. Phil's driving, looking for a quiet place to... well..."

Oborin glared up at Dubov. "You cocksucker."

"Yeah," Dubov said, "my boyfriend says I'm really good at it." He looked at Ari. "Is it an affront to, you know, female empowerment if I knock this fool out for you?"

"Be my guest."

"Just try it, you fa–"

Dubov punched him before he could finish what he was about to say.

Ari said, "Think he was going to say 'fabulous enforcer'?"

"Pretty sure, yeah." He ran a hand over his face. "Okay. What next?"

"Do you have a phone?"

He shook his head. "Coach made us leave them in the car."

"Shit. Okay, uh, what time is it?"

"Just after seven."

Ari nearly choked at the horror. She'd been incommunicado for over eight hours. Dale had to be absolutely terrified. There was nothing she could do about it yet, though. And calling at that moment to say she was safe would be a lie anyway. Better to wait.

"We'll deal with that once we're safe on shore. Oesterle said that the plan was to shoot me once they threw me overboard. That means they have a gun, right?"

"They have a couple, actually. None of them are loaded."

Ari said, "Why not?"

"I wasn't just sitting on my ass while they were planning your murder."

"Okay. Better for no one to have guns, I guess."

Dubov moved to the knocked-out men and dragged them into the corner. He reached for the handcuffs that had been holding Ari but stopped short when he saw they were still locked.

"How did you get out of these?"

"I have little hands."

He looked at her hands, looked at the cuffs, and then shook his head. "Well, I don't have the keys to them, so we'll have to find another way to tie them up."

"Sure. Okay."

She began searching through the drawers for anything that might be useful. "Once we've taken care of them, we need to get back to shore to call the authorities."

Dubov hesitated. "Yeah. About that... do you have any idea how to drive a boat?"

"How hard could it be?" she said. Dubov looked pained. "Okay. Yeah. But we'll worry about that later. Keep looking."

He nodded and continued his search.

CHAPTER TWENTY-ONE

LINDHOLM'S BOAT was more of a yacht. Ari remembered seeing it when she followed him for a day early in the case. The bridge on top of the cabin where they'd locked her up, enclosed on three sides but open at the back. She pushed the door open with her foot and peered out to confirm the ladder was where she thought it would be. Aulie, Oesterle, and Oborin had been secured with their belts and locked in the small bedroom at the back of the cabin. Dubov found the roofies in Oborin's pocket and slipped one to each man the same way they'd drugged Ari. She tried to feel guilty, tried to worry it might interact with the Cyn already in their systems, but she couldn't muster either emotion.

Lindholm and Muldoon were the only two threats left to deal with. Ari left the cabin with Dubov behind her. Muldoon's voice was echoing off the curved lines of the boat, joining with the thrum of the engine, so she knew to keep quiet as they made their climb. At the top of the ladder she moved quickly to the right and kept low. The bridge didn't have a door and she could see Lindholm and the coach standing together at the console. She pressed her back against the railing and waited. It was darker than it had been when she woke up, but there was still a chance it was bright enough Muldoon would notice her when he walked by.

Dubov had remained on the ladder. "Coach! She's bawling her eyes out. Says she wants to talk, but only if you'll spare her girlfriend."

Muldoon sighed. "Christ. Little girls doing a man's job..." He walked out of the bridge. "Are the others watching her?"

"Yeah," Dubov said.

"Well, get out of the way so I can~"

Dubov grabbed the front of Muldoon's windbreaker and pulled, twisting at the waist. His other hand was wrapped tightly around the ladder rail but he still almost fell with Muldoon. He let go and the coach shouted a curse as he was flung onto the lower deck. Ari ducked around the bridge doorway as Lindholm was spinning around. She had once been told that the actual punch was not as important as the placement of it, and she aimed at a spot on his jaw just behind his chin. He rocked back on his heels and she was close enough at that point to kick the side of his knee. He went down and she stepped behind him.

"You want to go down with the drug-pushing, roofie-pushing, attempted murdering coach, or do you want me to tell the cops you were cooperative? We can go either way and, frankly, I haven't gotten my fill of beating the shit out of you guys yet. So what do you say, Phil? Wanna be a hero?" She considered her choice of words. "Well... less of a villain than the rest of these guys, at least."

He nodded slowly.

"Good. You have the keys for the handcuffs you guys used on me?"

"Coach has 'em."

Ari looked at the ladder. Dubov had gone down the ladder to deal with Muldoon, and she could hear them scuffling down below.

"Tyler? You doing okay down there?"

He didn't respond, but she heard a punch land.

"Shit..."

Lindholm now had a choice. If Muldoon was winning, he could choose to remain loyal. They would outnumber her and he'd still come out on top.

"Tyler! You need a hand, buddy?"

"Don't worry about m..." He was cut off by the sound of a fist landing.

Ari looked at the console and reached out for the steering wheel. She grabbed it near the top curve and pulled down hard, turning the boat sharply to starboard. All the fragile human bodies onboard continued to obey the laws of physics. Ari and Lindholm were flung hard to the ground and fell away from each other. She heard the sound of two bodies falling on the deck below.

Lindholm spun around without rising from his belly. He reached out and grabbed her foot. Ari growled and brought her other foot up, slamming the sole of her shoe into the flat of his nose. Blood spurted down over his lips and he loosened his grip. She scrambled away from him and pushed herself up onto her hands and knees. Lindholm rushed her. Ari rolled to the side. He attempted to change trajectory at the last second but ended up losing his balance. He fell against the console and Ari punched him again. Her hand was throbbing like hell, the knuckles raw and wrist numb from all the thick skulls she'd been slamming them against, but Lindholm went down.

"Okay," he said. "Okay, okay, okay. I'll drive you back to shore."

Ari said, "That gun under the console doesn't have any bullets in it."

"What?"

His eyes betrayed him before he could catch himself. Ari reached under where he'd looked, grabbed the gun, and shook her head.

"You just lost your chance to surrender for real, Phil. On your feet."

"Good luck piloting this thing yourself."

Ari said, "Yeah, yeah, I'm sure we can figure something out."

He got up and touched his nose. He hissed and let her lead him toward the ladder. Muldoon and Dubov were grappling below. Muldoon had his back to the ladder. Ari's conscience poked her and told her that what she was thinking would be wrong, cruel, and bad sportsmanship. Then she remembered they had drugged her and planned to kill everyone she loved. That way she didn't feel so bad when she put her shoulder in the center of Lindholm's back and shoved him over the edge. He yelped as he fell so Muldoon turned in time to have his defenseman fall on top of him like a meteorite.

Dubov had seen what was happening and jumped back just in time. He checked to make sure they were both unconscious and then looked up at Ari with a smile on his face.

"You're kind of destructive, you know."

She shrugged. "They pissed me off. Tie those guys up. I'm going to see if I can teach myself how to drive a boat."

He chuckled and went to work.

Ari retrieved the handcuff keys from Muldoon's pocket and secured him to the wall. She gave him a roofie as well, but Lindholm was left semiconscious in a chair on-deck. Night had finally fallen and she had turned on the lights so she could see what she was doing. Dubov had his elbows on the railing, one foot crossed over the other with his fingers laced together as she made sure Lindholm was secured in place. Ari approached cautiously, very aware of the water rolling below. She put her hands on the rail but remained upright just in case there was a sudden shift in the boat's movement.

"It's okay," he assured her.

"Uh-huh. Do you even know where we are?"

He pointed at a cluster of lights across the water. "See that? That's Port Angeles."

She furrowed her brow and pointed. "I thought that was north..."

"No. Home is back that way." He hooked a thumb over his shoulder.

"Damn."

"You got hit in the head a lot. And you got drugged."

Ari said, "Right. Speaking of which." She passed him the pill bottle and wiped her hands in case handling the pills left residue. "I can't believe I'm actually feeling grateful for the date-rape drug."

Dubov said, "Even the vilest of things can have its purpose. I could keep knocking them out every time they wake up, but I think my knuckles would protest."

"Tell me about it." She flexed her hand. The knuckles were red and tender, and every movement of her fingers sent a weak protest of pain. "Thanks for the help back there."

"I'm the enforcer. I protect my team." He looked out at the water. "You're more my team than any of those bastards."

"Do you have any idea where Muldoon's iPad ended up?"

Dubov said, "Yeah. When they said that's what you grabbed, I made sure to keep track of it. Wait here." He went up onto the bridge and came back with the tablet.

Ari turned it on. Muldoon hadn't locked it, which she was grateful for, and a few seconds of searching led her to the right app. She smiled and ran her eyes down the columns.

"Purchases, hand-offs, debts owed. There are only initials, but that should be enough for the NHL to do a couple of drug tests." She double-checked and then breathed a sigh of relief. "No entries for T.D. You're off the hook, Tyler."

His eyebrows rose. "You thought I was a double agent? Even after I got my ass kicked by Muldoon for you? That's gratitude for ya."

"Hey, can't be too careful."

"Save a woman's life, get into a fight with my coach..." He shook his head and clucked his tongue as he leaned on the railing again. "It's enough to turn a guy off women completely."

Ari joined him. "I turned you off the whole gender, huh?"

"Well, that and a couple of other things."

She laughed, but it was weak. She had now been out of contact for ten hours. It had been years since she'd gone that long without speaking to Dale. Either a text or a phone call...

"You're really worried about your girl, huh?"

"Are you sure there isn't a phone or, or a radio or something onboard?"

He said, "Sorry. I patted everyone down when I tied them up, but I didn't find anything."

She tried not to think about the panic, the fear going through Dale's mind. Her hands were shaking so she linked the fingers and squeezed hard. Dubov reached over and put a hand on her back.

Lindholm grunted. Ari moved over to him, wiping at her eyes before she crouched down in front of him. She tilted her head so she could see his face.

"Hey. Sorry about that, but you were the only weapon I had at my disposal. And you had just tried to betray me. So I figure we can call it a wash. But you're the only person on this boat who hasn't been roofied, so you have that going for you." Dubov cleared his throat. "Oh, you and Tyler. It's still a pretty exclusive club. And I'm going to give you one more chance to do the right thing. You can pilot this boat back to shore where we can call the cops, or we can figure out how to get there ourselves. Either way you'll be going to jail. Choose the way that might get you a little sympathy."

He raised his head and looked past her. She moved to one side so he could see into the cabin.

"Yep, everyone's down for the count. I can give you a pill, too. You can go to sleep and wake up in custody, or you can surrender yourself like a good boy. Cops won't admit it, but they really like criminals who surrender. Those are the guys who always get offered the best deals."

He took a deep breath and closed his eyes. "I'll take us back to the dock."

She smiled. "Great. Tyler, will you take him up to the bridge? You'll tell Tyler how to get us home. I don't want to say you're untrustworthy, but I'd rather have you handcuffed for any time we're going to spend together."

Dubov hauled Lindholm to his feet and looked at the ladder. Ari watched as Dubov climbed the ladder with one hand while dragging Lindholm with the other. She wanted to enjoy it but, now that the danger was passed, all she could think about was getting home to Dale. She looked out at Port Angeles and knew she would be willing to jump overboard and swim over if she could be promised a cell phone and a fast cab waiting on the shore. She put her hand to her throat and touched the collar Dale had put on her.

"Just a little while longer, sweetie," she whispered. "I'm coming back, just a little while longer."

Dale was seated in Diana's car, watching as the Tukwila police examined the crime scene of Ari's car. Their car. The car they had bought together from a college girl going home to Idaho. The girl had seen Ari's collar and thought it was "kinky" and asked her out. Ari had smiled and said, "It actually means I'm taken." She looked at Dale and her smile grew. "It means I'm hers." She had unconsciously started playing with her bracelet, the custom-made piece of jewelry she'd had made to honor their connection. Strands of Ari's hair twined with fur from the wolf. Both sides of the woman she loved blended together, inseparable. She twisted it between her thumb and forefinger as if it was a talisman.

Dale closed her eyes and squeezed them tight to keep any tears from getting free. When she opened them she saw Diana walking back from her conversation with the local detective. She was almost at the car when her phone rang. She looked at the screen as Diana got in the car, but it showed up as an unknown number. She cleared her throat, sniffled, and answered.

"This is Dale."

"I'm okay. I'm coming home."

Dale put her free hand over her face and sobbed, her other hand clenching tight around the phone. She sagged forward until her forehead was almost touching the dashboard. Diana touched her hand softly before she eased the phone out of her grip.

"Ariadne?"

"Yeah. Is she okay?"

Diana put her hand on Dale's back and rubbed gently. "Yeah, she'll be fine. She's just a little overwhelmed hearing your voice. She was really worried about you." She put the phone on speaker. "Are you okay?"

"I'll be fine. I spent the last hour on a boat without any way of calling shore. I'm in Anacortes now, but I have to deal with the police here."

Dale wiped her face. "Anacortes?"

"Yeah, sweetie. It's going to be at least another couple of hours before I get home."

Diana said, "She'll stay with Lucy and me tonight."

Dale mouthed 'thank you' and Diana squeezed her hand.

"The guys you were investigating. Is that still going on?"

"No, they're all taken care of. That's part of the reason it's going to take a while with the police. I need to explain how I ended up on a boat with four roofied hockey players."

Dale said, "Lady drugs half the hockey team. Way to turn the tables, puppy."

"What can I say, I'm a trendsetter. Diana, can I talk to Dale?"

"Sure." She took the phone off speaker and handed it to Dale.

"Hi, puppy."

"I love you."

Dale closed her eyes. "I love you, too. So much, Ariadne. Swear you're okay. Tell me the god's-honest truth."

"I'm a little fuzzy-headed, weak, exhausted, sore as hell, but everything will heal. I could use one of those patented Dale Frye massages when I get home."

"You won't be able to keep my hands off of you."

Ari laughed. "I should go. The police want to talk to me."

"Okay. Ari... I'll marry you. Or whatever you want, whatever ceremony you decide feels right for us. Count me in."

"Done," Ari said. "Name a time and place and I'll be there. I'll even wear a dress for you."

Dale laughed. "I would've done it just to see that."

"I really have to go now. There's a police officer gesturing at the phone, and I don't think he has a sense of humor. Love you."

"I love you, too."

Dale hung up and wiped at her face. Diana rested a hand on her shoulder and squeezed. "Are you okay?"

"I'm fantastic," Dale said. "Just... emotional. Part of me wasn't sure." She swallowed the lump in her throat as she admitted that to Diana and herself at the same time. "But now. Now I'm okay."

"Good. I'm going to tell the local LEOs that we've found her. Then I'll take you home. We have a guest room so you won't have to suffer with the couch."

"Okay."

"And hey. I heard what you said. Lucy's going to terrorize you to be part of your bridal party."

Dale smiled. "Oh. Well, I'm sure~"

"Tell her no."

"What?"

"If anyone's going to be your matron of honor, it's going to be me."

"I think we can work something out."

Diana said, "Just remember who asked first. I'll be right back."

She got out of the car. Once she was alone, Dale wiped her face and then shook her hands as if she had just pulled all the anguish and worry from her skin. She looked at her phone and looked across the parking lot at their abandoned car. This time she smiled when she saw it. Some bastards had broken the window. They'd overpowered her, dragged her up the coast to Anacortes, apparently drugged her, threw her on a boat, and her puppy had still found a way to save herself. She couldn't help but laugh. She bumped her fist against her leg.

"Well done, Ariadne. Well-fucking-done."

She put her head back against the seat rest and closed her eyes as the relief washed over her. By the time Diana got back to the car, she was fast asleep.

CHAPTER TWENTY-TWO

DALE WOKE with a hand in her hair and lips on her cheek. She didn't open her eyes; she didn't want to see the exhaustion or bruises that were sure to be written all over her partner's face. Instead she freed her arms from the blanket and wrapped them around the familiar shape kneeling next to the bed. She rolled over and pulled Ari on top of her. Ari's lips moved from Dale's cheek to her lips and they kissed as Ari positioned herself more comfortably on top of her.

"What time is it?"

"Almost dawn. Go back to sleep."

"Are you all in one piece?" Dale said against the corner of Ari's mouth.

"Yeah."

"Good." She kissed Ari's mouth and whispered, "Good," again before letting herself fall back to sleep. She smiled because she could feel Ari's hand still in her hair.

Ari woke hungover and stiff, her every movement forced and painful. One of her grunts of pain woke Dale, who pushed off the blankets and climbed on top of her. "It's okay, puppy. I still remember the moves." She started at the shoulders and worked her way down Ari's arms. The massages had once been a necessity and part of her daily life. There were years when the only time she touched Ari's body was to soothe aching muscles. She'd learned her lover's body long before she ever kissed it or held it in her arms. Now she knew every inch intimately, and she smiled as her fingers slid over the smooth skin above Ari's elbow, up to her shoulder, and down the center of her back. She ignored the bruises she saw, though she noted each one with worry.

"Tell me what happened," Dale whispered.

Ari turned her head on the pillow and described what happened on the boat. Dale moved down the bed to continue her massage on Ari's legs.

"Dubov saved you?" she said when Ari finished her story.

"Yeah. I don't know what I would've done without him there."

"I want to meet him. The only thing I've seen from him are those godawful homophobic frat boy tweets. I want to respect him."

Ari rolled over. "You will. He wants to meet you, too. He thinks you must be something special for me to go ballistic the way I did."

Dale stretched out on top of her. They could hear Diana and Lucy elsewhere in the house. Ari dressed, her movements a bit looser thanks to Dale's ministrations, and they went out to join their friends for breakfast. Dale noticed that Ari was wearing a pair of acid-wash jeans and a baggy T-shirt, an odd outfit to be sure but not worth mentioning. When they got to the kitchen, Diana hugged Ari and made sure she was okay before inviting her to sit down and be served breakfast. Lucy was already seated, wearing a T-shirt with the Pride flag on it, but she stood up to hug Ari as well.

Diana served everyone scrambled eggs and bacon, with an extra portion for "the one who spent the night beating up junkie rapists." Ari repeated the story of what she'd been through for their benefit and cradled the mug of coffee Lucy poured for her like she'd been poisoned and it held the antidote.

"When we got back to Anacortes, I called the local cops to come gather up Muldoon and the others. Tyler and I gave our statements and they were charged with... hell, I don't even remember everything. Kidnapping and drugging me for a start. I'm sure everything else will get added on the deeper they investigate."

Diana said, "Drug tests?"

"I made sure the local cops knew they should get that done as soon as possible, but I don't know if they went with it. Cyn stays in the system for a couple of days, so hopefully it'll show up no matter when they get tested. And even if they don't, I have a list of purchases going back to the week Muldoon came to Seattle. He had a list of players he wanted and, as soon as they were brought into the team, he started pushing the Cyn on them."

"Why just those four?" Lucy asked. "Why not the whole team?"

Dale said, "Did you see how expensive that drug is? Those may have been the only players who could afford it."

Ari said, "And there's the fact that if your entire team is playing like Captain America, the NHL might smell something rotten. So he got two of his forwards and two defensemen to act as the ringers. I get the feeling everyone on the team is going to be getting a drug test as soon as possible."

Diana sighed. "Well, that's an auspicious start for Seattle's new major league sports team."

Ari nodded. "After I got everything settled, I asked if I was free to go and they told me to keep in touch. Muldoon had taken my wallet and phone back at the arena, so I didn't have any reason to keep my clothes, so I just..." She shrugged.

Lucy said, "You turned into the wolf?"

"None of the car rental places were open, I didn't have money to pay them with anyway, I didn't feel like having someone call me an Uber. I wasn't going to call someone to come get me. When I got back, I raided one of my stashes that isn't far from here and got dressed. It's only about eighty miles." Ari reached out and laced her fingers with Dale's. "I was inspired to get back as soon as possible."

Lucy put her elbows on the table and cupped her face with both hands, smiling goofily. "That's so romantic."

Diana said, "What's next?"

"Now I have to go to give my report to Cecily Parrish. I'll tell her what happened and she can report to the owner that he has to replace some people." She looked at Dale. "And then I'll tell her I'm done with her. Completely, one hundred percent out. No more retainer, no more hoops."

Dale smiled. "Good."

"Is there a bus stop nearby? I obviously need to go home and change clothes first."

Lucy waved her off. "You can take my car until you get yours back. I'm working from home today, nowhere to be."

"Are you sure?"

"Absolutely."

Ari said, "I'm not sure how us volunteering to be your

chauffeur turned into us taking your car, but I appreciate it. I won't keep it longer than necessary."

Dale said, "I'll look into rentals while you're cutting us loose from GG&M."

"That works."

"I'll get the keys for you," Diana said. "After breakfast. I went to all the trouble of cooking for you, so you're going to enjoy the meal."

Ari leaned toward Lucy. "Is she always this strict?"

"Mm-hmm." She smiled at her wife. "And I wouldn't have it any other way."

The doors parted to reveal a handful of suits standing inside the elevator. One of the passengers stepped forward and smoothed a hand over the side of her hair before she approached the receptionists. Her suit was dark grey polyester, a blazer and matching skirt that reached past her knees. The strap of her messenger bag crossed her chest, and the bag rested comfortably against her hip as she walked just a bit unsteadily on high heels. She was indistinguishable from any of the other automatons she'd seen since entering the building and she struggled to keep from squirming.

A young woman who didn't look old enough to have graduated high school smiled up at her. "Welcome to Gilles Girard & Moreau. How may I help you?"

"Miss Ariadne Willow to speak with Cecily Parrish, if you please."

Shannon's replacement smiled. "I'll let her know you're here. If you would have a seat..."

"Certainly."

Ari walked to the waiting area and sat down. She picked up a copy of *Grist* and slowly read through it. She started checking her phone after eleven minutes. At forty-five minutes she finished the magazine and considered that possibility that Cecily was testing her. She picked up another magazine and started it from the beginning.

Ninety minutes after her arrival, Cecily appeared. "Miss Willow. I trust you weren't kept waiting too long."

Ari gave her a pinched smile as she put the magazine back. "Not long at all."

Cecily smiled and gestured for Ari to lead the way back into the offices. "You look quite lovely today, Miss Willow. Very professional."

Ari was close enough to whisper, "Shove it up your ass," quietly enough that only Cecily could hear it.

Cecily walked beside her. "See how smoothly things go when you play by the rules?"

"This isn't a surrender. If anything, I'm patronizing your little ritual about waiting at the gates." She pushed through the door of Cecily's office. "This is the last time I'll be gracing your little corner of the world with my presence, so I thought I might as well make it official."

"Last time?"

"I'm closing the Totems case." She opened her bag and handed Cecily a manila envelope. "This contains a flash drive with copies of everything I found, plus printouts of the same. Generic background on most players. The majority of them were clean. Chuck Weaver was picked up for marijuana possession when he was sixteen. If it's still a problem, it won't matter now that pot is legal here."

Cecily took the folder and walked around her desk. "Very impressive."

"I also should inform you that Conor Muldoon, Steve Aulie, Kristof Oborin, Phillipe Lindholm, and Anton Oesterle are currently being held by the Anacortes Police Department on a handful of fun charges that I've listed in the file. You're probably going to advise Mr. Levitt to replace those gentlemen as soon as possible."

Cecily had opened the file and skimmed the top page. "Kidnapping? Who did they kidnap?"

"That would be me. The attempted murder was also me. And the drugging, the assault, et cetera. I detailed the incidents for you."

"I see. Well, you seem to have certainly gone above and beyond for this case. I'll see that payroll cuts you a check before you leave."

Ari nodded. "I appreciate that, Miss Parrish. You might also want someone to start the paperwork showing that I've resigned from... whatever the hell you had me doing. Was it still probation? Whatever you want to call it, I'm done."

Cecily sat down. "That's a bold decision."

"It's been a long time coming. I realized every argument I made was justifying the job. Telling myself I should take it and then forcing myself to come up with reasons why it made sense. That should've told me I didn't want it. I don't care about the extra money if it means doing a job I don't like and working for someone

I don't respect."

"I'm prepared to amend the offer," Cecily said. "This is another big win for the firm, Miss Willow. The two cases you've worked for us have been extremely lucrative. Ike Levitt is a huge client and your discoveries are bound to make him very happy. I'm prepared to offer you carte blanche. You stay at your little office on Belmont, you keep Miss Frye, you get the big paycheck from the prestigious law firm. In return, you occasionally take cases like this one."

"Nice simple cases that end with me handcuffed and roofied on a boat full of men? Yeah, no thanks. Besides, that doesn't really address the whole 'boss I don't respect' thing."

Cecily took a deep breath and let it out slowly. "That's disappointing. But I suppose I have done everything I can to entice you."

Ari said, "If it's all the same to you, I'll wait for the check at reception. There are a couple of magazines I didn't get a chance to read during your little power play. Best of luck with your future endeavors. I know we're most likely going to see each other at the trial if I have to testify, but don't expect us to go out for lunch afterward."

"Miss Willow." Cecily stood up. "You may think I'm your enemy, but I assure you that isn't the case. I am your friend. I only tried to make these offers of employment as... generous for you as possible. I hope you understand that."

"Sure," Ari said. "You're nothing but kind, Miss Parrish. A total giver. I'll see you in court, but hopefully not for very long."

She felt Cecily's eyes on her as she left the office, but she refused to look back. Part of her wanted to just keep going, but the check was too huge to just throw it away. She'd suffered far too much on the case to walk away from it. She'd spend Cecily Parrish's money as easily as any other check she'd earned, but she would be glad to be done with GG&M. She wasn't the sort to work in a high-rise downtown, to wear power suits and high heels just to fit in on the elevator. She and Dale built Bitches into a place where they could be themselves, where they could be comfortable. Something like that was precious, and from that point on, she was going to remember that.

Chapter Twenty-Three

A MONTH later, Ari and Dale received a package from Tyler Dubov that contained two tickets to the official Seattle Totems announcement. Ari paid for two extra tickets and invited Diana and Lucy to come along as a thank-you for their help. The morning of the announcement, Dale came out of the shower to find Ari sitting on the edge of their bed. "Puppy. Can you do up my bracelet?"

"Sure." Dale approached and offered her arm. Ari bent over the wrist and carefully snapped the clasp. Once it was in place she brought the hand up and kissed Dale's pulse point before letting it go. "There you are."

Dale watched Ari's face. "You don't have to marry me."

Concern passed over Ari's face. "I know it's taking me a while to think of the right way to do it, but I'm just looking for the exact right thing."

Dale crouched and cupped Ari's cheeks. "I know. But that's just it. We don't need the right way to do it. You have your collar, I have my bracelet. Why do we need a ceremony? As far as I'm concerned, you're mine and I'm yours. Everything we've been through together. All I need is this little reminder of you and your wolf. And every time we get pulled apart, we find each other. We save each other. We stand by each other. You almost changed your entire life because of my place in it. I think that's all the proof anyone needs that you're in this for the long haul. Now, if you're dead-set on me having your name..."

"No." Ari's voice was quiet because of the effort it was taking her not to cry. "No, I hate that whole thing."

"Good. Me too." She kissed Ari. "It just hit me that maybe the reason we couldn't figure out the right way to commit to each other was because we already did it. We've been married a long time, puppy. We just didn't realize it."

"Yeah," Ari said. "So... if you're not my girlfriend, and we're not officially wives..."

"I'm your mate."

Ari raised an eyebrow and then laughed. "I don't think that will work around people who don't know I'm a wolf."

"So in private or with your mom or friends, we're mates. To everyone else... partner."

"I can live with partner. Come here."

Dale climbed onto Ari's lap, and Ari fell back onto the bed. Later on she blamed the fact that Dale was only wearing a towel, which made access easier, while Dale insisted Ari wouldn't have been stopped by a suit of armor.

Whoever was to blame, they were late picking up their friends for the carpool.

Ari expected a dry press conference featuring the media snapping pictures of managers and owners as the team awkwardly filed onto a stage set up on the ice. Instead they arrived at the Tukwila arena to find huge crowds filling the lobby, transforming the empty echo chamber where Muldoon and his cronies had captured her to an actual sports venue. Posters with the team's logo and name were hung up everywhere she turned, with banners hanging over every entrance.

When Ari handed over her tickets, the man at the door checked something and ushered her to the side. He spoke with someone in a STAFF polo shirt and they were ushered away.

"Uh, our friends," Ari said, trying not to be separated from the Macallans.

Diana waved her to go on. "We'll meet you at our seats."

Ari reluctantly went along with being escorted out of the public area and into one of the dark, narrow hallways she'd last seen while being pursued by the former players who were now sitting in a jail cell awaiting trial. Dale seemed to know where they were and wrapped an arm around her elbow. Ari smiled and patted her hand. They could hear the dull rumble of people moving in other parts of the building, the thud of feet on bleachers and the hum of voices echoing off brick and concrete.

They arrived at the locker room and were told to wait by the door. The staffer went inside and, a few seconds later, emerged with Tyler Dubov. He was fully geared up for the event, and he had a pair of jerseys draped over his right arm.

"Tyler! Dale, this is~"

"The man who saved your life." Dale had already let go of Ari to wrap her arms around Dubov's neck. She looked miniscule next to him, thanks to his height and the extra bulk provided by his gear. She had to stand on her toes to reach, but she managed. "Thank you."

He smiled bashfully. "After what she did for me, it's the least I could've done. I wanted to be sure I saw you two before this whole thing happened. I wanted you to have the first official merch for the Totems." He held up one of the jerseys and twisted it to show the back. Instead of the typical white lettering, DUBOV 36 was filled in with rainbow colors. "I, ah, asked if some of the merchandise could be connected to Pride. They said sure, no problem. So..."

Ari laughed and took the jersey. "This is amazing. So you're officially out?"

"On the way," he said, sighing nervously. "It's a big process. The guys already know, of course. New coach. The owner. It was like you said. Seattle is a good place to be an out athlete. We're doing a big public thing just to get it out of the way in a week or so."

Dale said, "Congratulations."

"I owe it to your girl here. Without her, I'd still be hiding. And I'd be playing on a team with rapists and junkies."

"The new guys are better?"

"The new guys are fantastic. We're a stronger team without the guys you took down. The coach is a great guy, too. He supported the idea of the Pride merchandise."

Ari said, "It's going to go over great in this town. Would you sign it?"

Dubov grinned. "I thought you'd never ask."

He signed both jerseys, accepted another hug from Dale, and then had to go back to finish getting ready. The staffer escorted Dale and Ari back through the bowels of the arena to their seats, where Diana and Lucy were already waiting. Ari had put on her jersey and turned so they could see the colors. Lucy was jealous, and Diana promised to buy her one as soon as they became available.

The announcement ceremony opened with a performance by Femme Reapers. Dale fanned Ari's face as the duo walked out onto a special stage at center ice. They wore their trademark dusters but, underneath, they were wearing Totems jerseys. They performed a song called "Hit Somebody!" by Warren Zevon. Ari loved it because the song told the story of a noble enforcer, a man whose only job on the ice was to protect his team. The player in the song did his job for twenty years, but he never stopped dreaming of making a goal. The triumphantly tragic ending of the song had everyone on their feet by the time an emcee came out to introduce the team.

Each player took the ice as their name was called. Ari stood and whistled for Dubov, and he held his stick above his head when he spotted her. She and Dale both cheered for him as he circled around the join the rest of the team. Ari sat back down and linked their arms together. Dale had worried about being too cold before they arrived, so she put an arm around her. Dale snuggled closer and put her head on Ari's shoulder.

When they got back to the office, there would be a lot of work to do. They were currently working three cases, an attempt to keep their bank account on the right side of solvent. The tickets for Diana and Lucy had been extravagant but they agreed it was necessary to show their gratitude. They'd also agreed to buy a new car to replace the one that had been broken into. It was time to say goodbye to the car anyway and it made sense to upgrade to something newer. Now that they couldn't count on the retainer from GG&M, even with their savings, money was going to be a bit tight.

Ari didn't care. She'd work five cases at once if she had to. The money they brought in might be meager, but it would be honest. It wouldn't come with whatever strings Cecily Parrish might attach to her paycheck from the law firm. She rubbed Dale's arm and kissed the top of her head, smiling as the players split into two teams for a quick exhibition game.

Whatever happened with the agency, they were going to come by it honestly or not at all. She wouldn't have it any other way.

It was past dark when Cecily's headlights swept across the face of her home. The living room lights were on, as were the twin sconces on either side of the front door. She gathered her things and climbed out of the car. It had been an agonizingly dull day of testimony and depositions. She'd been forced to take the new secretary into her office just to break up the monotony. It hadn't worked. She was still frustrated enough to mentally thumb through her contact list for someone she could call over. Maybe she would call two or three someones for some variety.

She unlocked her door and went inside, crossing halfway to the stairs before she realized someone was in her living room. She stopped and rested her hand on the newel, bowing her head without turning around. She didn't know which of the partners it would be, but none of them would be preferable to the other two.

"I thought I asked you not to enter my home without permission again."

"You would presume to give us orders?" She recognized the voice as Moreau's.

"No, I simply~"

He interrupted. "You promised us a wolf."

Cecily didn't look toward him. The fingers of one hand curled around the handle of her briefcase while the other tightened on the newel. She focused on a random spot on the hardwood floor in front of her. She steadied her breath so her words wouldn't tremble when she spoke.

"It's proven more complicated than I thought."

"When a promise is made, we expect you to follow through with it. Certainly after all this time, you have come to understand that."

Cecily said, "Of course I do. But the very qualities that you admire in the wolf are making this an impossible request. Her compassion, loyalty, and resolve are the very reasons she won't abandon her agency to work for us. She is devoted to her partner and the business they've built together."

Moreau was closer when he spoke again. "We can be patient. But that patience has a limit. This wolf is special. She stalled a war which has been waged for hundreds of years. She has been able to maintain a relationship with a non-wolf. She intrigues us. She would be an invaluable asset."

Her skin crawled. "I'm well aware of the stakes," Cecily said, her voice meek and nearly whispered. "I shall do everything in my power to convince her that she should join our ranks."

"If she will not see reason, desperate measures will have to be taken. If she will not abandon her business, destroy it. If she refuses to abandon her partner, then her partner will have to be taken out of the equation. The relationship doesn't matter so much as the woman who made it work. She is our prize, Cecily Parrish, and we will have her."

Cecily nodded. "Of course, Mx. Moreau. Thank you for giving me another chance."

Moreau didn't respond, but she felt the brush of air as he passed by behind her. She suppressed a shudder as she listened to the door open and then click shut. The tension left her body and nearly made her collapse, but she maintained her grip on the bannister to remain upright. There hadn't been a car waiting outside so she didn't know how Moreau had gotten there or how he planned to get home, but she couldn't care less. She smoothed her hands over her clothes to disguise the fact her hands were shaking.

Perhaps she wouldn't entertain after all. She felt a sudden urge to be alone for the rest of the night. A nice long bath and then meditation before bed sounded like just the thing she needed.

She left her briefcase in the foyer and undressed on her way upstairs. She would get Ariadne Willow to work for them. Kindness hadn't worked and intimidation had destroyed any forward progress she had made. Perhaps the time had come to resort to cruelty. It wasn't an ideal tactic, but one couldn't be choosy in times as desperate as these.

The only thing she knew for certain was that failure would not be an option. Ariadne would agree or she would suffer the consequences of refusal.

ABOUT THE AUTHOR

Geonn Cannon lives in Oklahoma. He is the author of several novels, including the Riley Parra series which is currently being produced as a webseries for Tello Films, and an official Stargate SG-1 tie-in novel. Information about his other novels and an archive of free stories can be found online at geonncannon.com.